XERN:
The Exile

XERN: THE EXILE

First edition. May 28, 2024.

Copyright © 2024 Todd Parker.

ISBN: 979-8224618989

Written by Todd Parker.

Table of Contents

Many thanks to Erin Ayles who encouraged me along the way and gave me feedback. This is what she says about this book:

"Love. Sacrifice. Intrigue. Secrets. A world of mystery and jeopardy. Oh, and did I mention the main characters are Dragons? This book takes you into a unique society, where humans are an afterthought and Dragonkind are in charge. Then you are thrown into a new world, one where it is easy to make a fatal mistake."

Book 1 of Dragon Rule
The races of Xern

Dragons – Rulers of the known lands of Xern for the last several thousand Centa. Dragons used to be able to fly several thousand Centa ago but their wings no longer support flight. They detest Wingdits so much they have erased them from their knowledge (except for a few). Dragons used to fight Wingdits for control & to rule over them, but 1500 Centa ago it was decided it was not worth the losses to continue the battles & they are now left to their territory as long as they don't stray from it. Super-secret outposts are maintained for this purpose.

Wingdits – Tolerated race that most dragons don't even know about. They are a cross between dragons & humans. They are much taller than humans & shorter than dragons. They do have wings & can fly but prefer not to. They are consigned to a small territory in the desert. They have the form of humans but with wings & much larger.

Humans – the least of all the races & barely above the other life forms on Xern. Dragons detest them but they do make good laborers when they are kept busy.

Prologue

In the intervening Centa since the dragons had taken control of Xern, life had gone on smoothly. Humans had been placed in subjection to the dragons and were placed in "compounds" from which they were never to stray. Symb had ruled for the last 150 Centa. Prior to Symb's rule humans had been killed at will by the dragons, but Symb had put a stop to this realizing that humans where being killed faster than they could breed. This would eventually wipe out the dragon's workforce and so he had decreed in his great wisdom that no humans where to be killed by any dragon without his consent.

Still some dragons persisted in their old and careless ways. Rarely were dead humans ever found, but they just seemed to vanish without a trace. Thus about 50 Centa ago Symb formed the Shadow Dragons to root out the continuing disregard for his decree. After Symb, Shadow Dragons possessed the most power in Xern and were also like the shadows on a wall (where they really there?).

There was no night on Xern the blue orb simply ran in an oval path from the top of the sky to near the horizon & back again simply called a Turning. 100 Turnings made up a Centa. Humans lived for about 20 or 30 Centa while dragons lived for about 500 Centa.

Chapter 1 - The Exile

He gazed into her blue crystalline eyes. For several minutes neither one moved then Parthen had enough of this human. How dare he look at a dragon like this! She knew that as part of the Dragon Guard she should simply return him to the compound. But she had enough of these humans and in an instant blue flame enveloped him & he was reduced to ashes.

She knew this was against the rules laid out by Symb but she didn't care he would never know nor miss yet another human. She also knew rain was coming & would wash the ashes away removing all trace of him. She moved on in her daily rounds of the forest surrounding the compound.

Each day the Dragon Guard would go about their assigned routes around the compound making sure no humans strayed from their assigned work. Most days were uneventful & Parthen enjoyed being out alone experiencing all that Xern had to offer. Humans had learned, though rather slowly Parthen thought, to stay within their assigned areas & not wander off. She thought Symb had made the humans bolder though with his demanding that no humans be killed. She could remember her mother saying that back in her day she would go an entire Centa without seeing a human wandering off!

Furto, member of the Shadow Dragons, followed close behind Parthen, she knew nothing of his presence. He had been assigned to watch her as her movements had come under suspicion. The Shadow Dragons were an elite & secret group that only Symb knew about. Their mission was to watch & collect evidence on the lesser dragons should they veer from Symb's orders.

Furto had been following Parthen for many turnings now. As he had twice before Furto carefully collected the ashes in his evidence bag then caught up with Parthen. He knew her path would take them near the great river shortly where he would dispose of the evidence as he had before.

He loved Parthen, she was beautiful with rare blue crystalline eyes that swirled mesmerizing him. Her scales were a lovely deep blue & he had come to appreciate her distain for the humans. She did not know he loved her or even existed for that matter but he could not turn her in to his commander. This was a dangerous game he was playing and he knew the consequences of being found out. Symb was not one to be messed with; he knew no mercy when his commands were broken! Yet how could he turn in the one he had come to love so deeply?

She continued down the trail enjoying the birds and life of the forest. The trail led next to the river and she stopped for a bit to relax next to the babbling water. He watched her from the shadows desperately wishing he could reveal himself – but that would spell the end of any Shadow Dragons career. He too enjoyed the wildlife of Xern. It was so rich & vibrant here everywhere he looked there was life of some kind crawling, walking or flying. O how he wished dragons could fly again! Maybe someday dragonkind would find the answer to that question!

After she moved on, he took the evidence bag & carefully rinsed it to making sure no a spot of ash was left in it, then blowing with ever so slight flame to dry it out. Once again, he hurried on to catch up with Parthen.

Later that evening he returned back to the compound after having followed her all day. He turned in his evidence bag, empty as usual and found his loft in Shadow Dragons secret compound. He was tired and went fast asleep.

Parthen having returned early told her commander that all was quiet on her route and she had encountered nothing out of the ordinary. Her commander had become suspicious of her some time ago as other Dragon Guard on her route always encountered humans that had wandered off the compound. But he chose to say nothing as she was highly regarded by her fellow Dragon Guard.

Parthen was the daughter of a prestigious line of dragons. Her mother was well known on Xern both for her tireless work for the leaders of dragonkind & because she was of royal blood. Her daughter was liked & well-spoken of by the rest of the Dragon Guard – but he often wondered if that was simply because of her lineage.

Early the next morning she was awakened by the sound of the Royal Guard entering the Dragon Guard sleeping quarters – they were a rather noisy bunch she thought. They were among the strongest of dragonkind and arrayed in purple garments with golden shields & gold & silver gilded swords. They were an imposing sight for any dragon to behold!

"Where is Parthen?" They demanded of her commander.

"Who is it that asks" He replied politely knowing full well who they were!

"You know who we are commander" they replied gruffly. They did not take kindly to dragons wasting their time! Their attitude was something to be desired she thought.

"Now bring her to us. Symb has ordered she be brought to the great hall this morning!"

"Get her yourselves" her commander replied. He pointed toward her. This surprised her as he could be in trouble for replying to them in such a manner. But as the Royal Guard moved in her direction without any further words, she suspected she was in real trouble if they ignored that insult! As they approached, she pretended to sleep on not moving the slightest. Being called to the great hall could not be a good thing! She had done nothing noteworthy and therefore it could only be a bad sign.

"You!!" The nearest of the three Royal Guard poked her with the tip of his sword.

"Get up Symb has demanded your presence this morning. You will come with us!"

Parthen popped open an eye then moved her tail and stretched her neck as if just waking up. She would not let them bully her with their fear tactics! Did they know who her mother was? She suspected not.

"What? What is this all about?" She said as if confused.

"We don't take messages we just follow orders. You can ask all you want when you get there, though it's probably better if you don't." They replied gruffly. She knew full well that they knew what this was about. They would not have passed up her commander's insult if they had not known. But she had learned from her mother that sometimes it was better to keep quiet then to question the Royal Guard.

They grabbed her arm rather roughly she thought and pulled her up.

"Okay let me go I will come with you. You don't have to be so rough" she replied irritated.

Meanwhile in the Shadow Dragons quarters Furto had been called to his commander. Early morning in the Shadow Dragon quarters, the others were hustling about getting ready for their daily missions. His good friend in the Shadow Dragons stopped & asked him how things were. They exchanged a few words before Furto went to see the Commander.

"Furto your presence has been requested in the great hall. You are to be there in 1 hr."

"Yes commander! What is this about, may I ask?"

"I am sorry Furto I cannot tell you that information."

This was not good he thought. Anytime that information was withheld from any member of the Shadow Guard it was always bad news for them. Have they found out about my evidence bag he thought, but how could they, it was washed clean! Furto was in good standing with Symb & they knew each other well. He hoped whatever happened this would buy him some good will.

An hour later he entered the great hall as had been requested and his hearts stopped – there sat Parthen on the judgment pedestal! He knew what he had to do but did he have the strength? Symb saw him enter.

"Furto! Exalted Shadow Dragon, come forward!"

A Shadow Dragon is never named in public unless it means the end of their career. He knew his was over at this point. He wondered what lay ahead. Before Parthen he saw his evidence bag - that could not be good. He glanced around and saw other members of the Shadow Guard around the room and his commander next to Parthen. He saw Jabas there too, apparently a large contingent of the Shadow Guard had been called to witness and this was not uncommon. But he wondered if they knew what was going. He had been a witness many times in the past. Sometimes they were told, sometimes they were not.

"Furto" his commander began.

"It has come to our attention that you are suppressing evidence. Last night when you returned your evidence bag was sent to the lab. It returned that there were traces of human ash caught in its seams. What do you have to say about this?"

He was grateful at least that as a member of the Shadow Guard he was given more leeway to answer any charges brought against him then other dragons were. Still, this was a very serious charge and he knew what the consequences of it were. He knew that he could easily implicate Parthen in this and at least save himself but he loved her too much to do that. The tricky part here was he did not know what Parthen may have already said. It is best in these circumstances to reply as little as possible short but to the point.

He replied "Yes that is human ash you have found in there."

The chamber went to a hushed silence – for all the dragons there knew what he was saying.

The commander continued – "Did you kill this human Furto? You know that Symb has decreed that dragons are not to kill humans!" He was not on the best terms with his commander, but still given Furto's relationship with Symb his commander had to tread carefully in his accusations.

Furto glanced at Symb who was intently looking at him. He was a fearsome dragon to behold surrounded by the splendid & fearsome Royal Guard! No wonder no dragon dared cross him! He had once thought of joining the Royal Guard but felt the Shadow Dragons better suited him!

"My most exalted commander – yes it was I who killed this human. I have fallen in love with Parthen who doesn't even know I exist and yet I have defended her three times when humans crossed the boundary and were trailing her"

At these words he saw Jabas out of the corner of his eye leave the chamber head bowed. He wondered if Jabas would ever speak to him again. There he said it. Maybe if Symb thought he was defending another dragon it would buy him some sympathy, but he doubted it. Parthen looked at him as he said these words. She seemed to have a look of distain in her eyes. No matter he had said his piece. The room went deathly silent as he replied to the commander.

"Furto – come here and stand next to Parthen" the commander said. Furto did as he was asked.

"Furto, we know what you just told is not entirely true. Dragons must at all times tell the truth! We know that you in fact did NOT kill the human. The ash was made from blue flame not your black flame. We further know that Parthen does in fact have blue flame. Besides all that Parthen has admitted to killing the human. You know the consequences for her and for you. She will be committed to the flame pit and you will be stripped of your rank."

Furto bowed his head in sorrow at these words. So, they had already examined her & apparently could tell more from the ash then he knew! Maybe that was just a rouse though. No matter it was all said & done now.

"NO!" Furto heard himself say. "I will take her place in the flame pit, if you save her life."

This caused an uproar in the great hall. Never before in his lifetime had any dragon offered to take the place of another! In dragonkind this was not done! Every dragon paid for their own transgressions! The shocked look on his commander told him everything.

"SILENCE" Symb commanded. And instantly the hall was quiet.

"My lord" Furto's commander said, but was cut off by Symb.

"Furto exalted Shadow Dragon - I have never seen such devotion in all my Centas here in the great hall. I do not know what you see in this one but here is my decision on this matter..." Well, that was different – a Shadow Dragon was never called a Shadow Dragon after being publicly named, much less exalted!

"Furto and Parthen will not be committed to the fire pit, both will be stripped of their ranks and both will be sent to the Yukla desert beyond the western boundary. They will be exiled there together - forever to live out their lives."

Chapter 2 - Furto

The Yukla desert is so barren & dry thought Furto. After the Shadow Guard had dropped them off Parthen had taken off on her own and told him in no uncertain terms not to follow her. He had given up everything for her and she had gone off on her own. He had not seen her since then nor did he expect to though he wished for it. It had been 20 Turnings now and he wondered how she was doing or even if she still lived. This desert could be so harsh. Nothing with any intelligence lived out here. Oh how he longed for another dragon to speak with! He was beginning to wonder if he was losing his mind.

Daily he went about the task of trying to survive; he was always hungry with little food to fill his stomach. The desert provided little for his large appetite. The little cave he found was actually quite nice and had a little stream nearby so he had enough water anyway & protection from the desert sun. At least he was thankful for that. But this just existing was not what dragons were born for, it was a fate worse than death. Dragons were born to rule not exist!

Several times over the past 20 Turnings he had ventured over to the eastern edge of the Yukla desert but each time he found the boundary guarded. Symb was taking no chances with him getting back in. The Shadow Guard were always watching, many of them he had patrolled with but now everything was different and they regarded his approach with distain in their eyes. He always looked for his friend Jabas, but he never saw him there. Again, Symb was taking no chances. With sadness he always returned to his cave bereft of everything that mattered to him. He often wondered why be bothered to go on with his miserable existence.

Not only had he lost everything that mattered, he had been stripped of his rank and exiled, but what he did it all for had left him alone. It seemed like he had given up everything that mattered and gained nothing in return. She did not even want him around her! He wondered if he should have just blamed her. They would have believed him and at least he would still be in the Shadow Guard. What was he thinking!! He loved her could not do that! He shook this thought out of his head!

He closed his eyes and saw her swirling blue eyes in his dreams. Maybe tomorrow he would go and just see if she was alright. He had told himself this a dozen times but had not yet done it. What held him back? Fear? Fear of her or maybe fear of than finding out the worst and he didn't want that after everything else that had happened! Still, he knew he should go looking for her and make sure she was okay. Tomorrow, yes tomorrow he would set out!

The next morning, he awoke – well today was the day he would go & look for Parthen! Best find something to eat before setting out. He looked out from his "home" & saw some Phons scurrying about. Well, they weren't much but they would have to do. He grabbed several & swallowed them whole while they screamed in protest! Damn noisy little creatures! Maybe if he found her, he could just observe unseen, after all as a member of the Shadow Guard stealth was something he excelled at in spite of his large size. Just to make sure she was okay.

He would first head over to the eastern edge of the Yukla desert and see if possibly the Shadow Guard there would talk to him. He wanted to find out if they had seen her at all since their exile here. Maybe just maybe he could get a bit of information from them that would help him. As he plodded on over to the border, he wondered what he would say. He was almost there now he better think of something!

As he crossed the last hill & looked down – it seemed strangely quiet. Then he saw a solitary Shadow Guard down on the edge. Very strange he thought usually there was a half dozen of them here. He looked carefully around, but indeed there was only one guard. As he got closer, he looked & thought that it looked like Jabas his closest friend in the Shadow Dragons. Luck is on my side today he thought! But another thought crossed his mind, Jabas had never before been there – why was he here now alone? Something did not sit right with him about this.

As he approached him Jabas, who was also black scaled as all Shadow Dragons were, turned and faced him. His eyes were not friendly but neither were they harsh, as so many others had been over the past months. He must be careful with what he said; he could use a friend right now. His eyes locked with Jabas's eyes and for a moment they both froze. Nothing was said but Furto felt him.

"Jabas" Furto said quietly with respect due a Shadow Dragon. Jabas nodded slightly and raised the tip of his tail. This was a private sign they created between themselves a long time ago. It meant they were alone and could speak freely.

"Jabas, has there been any sightings of Parthen? Has she been to the border here at all since our exile?" Furto asked.

"There have been no sightings of her Furto, she has not been here since the exile. It has been presumed she met up with you later on."

"No, I have no seen her since the day of our exile and now I am going in search of her. I was hoping to gather some information before I left."

"If I may ask, why are you here alone Jabas? I usually see many of the Shadow Guard here"

"I was sent here three Turnings ago on a special errand from Symb himself awaiting your return to the border, when that is complete the usual guard will resume." Jabas continued "Symb has relented in this one thing" Jabas motioned and a human appeared from behind the distant tree.

"Symb sends you this human to assist you in whatever tasks you have need of him for. No other dragons know of this mission, which is why I am alone."

Furto bowed and his eyes gleamed as a sign of respect and gratitude.

"Come" Jabas gruffy commanded him. The human came quickly.

"Is there one also for Parthen if she be found" Furto asked.

"No, Symb has no such sympathy for her Furto"

"Please convey my gratitude to Symb for me Jabas, I am sorry he does not feel as I do to Parthen."

Jabas nodded. "I wish you well my old friend" With that Jabas gave Furto a slight bow of respect. Strange thought Furto, he is my dearest friend but no dragon no matter how dear a friend shows respect however slightly to dragon stripped of his rank! Furto tucked this away in his mind for future thought.

Furto motioned to the human who came running quickly after him as he set out in the desert in the direction Parthen had gone 20 Turnings ago. The human was adequate if not a little scrawny but anything out here was better than nothing. He instructed the human in their simple language that he must keep up with him – he would not wait for him if he could not keep up. The human's eyes widened at this, but he nodded his head vigorously. He wondered if the human would be a help or hindrance to him. He did not want to waste any time looking for Parthen and would not tolerate any delays in his search. If he ever came back to Symb's presence however, without the human gift, that could be seen as an affront. He certainly hoped that would not be forever as Symb had proclaimed it to be. But He had never known a dragon to ever go back on his word.

About two Turnings out on his search he saw an unusual scratch on a rock it appeared to be made by a dragon claw but what it meant was a mystery to him. He hoped that meant he was going in the right direction! Had Parthen been in some danger? He would never forgive himself for not following her if he found out she had died or been attacked because he did not follow her immediately. He had to put this thought out of his mind and concentrate on the search! The human was absolutely useless in trying to figure this out & he didn't even ask him about it. Their power of reasoning was so weak it made him laugh at the thought!

He continued on with the strange scratching becoming more prevalent. He figured she must have gone this way because these marks could only be left by a dragon's claw. They seemed to be leading him or someone anyway but to where Furto had no idea. As far as he knew (and he was trained to know EVERYTHING!) there was nothing out here! By the end of the third turning the marks had become common enough to follow as trail markers. Still, he was mystified as to what this all meant. He was certain now that Parthen was not kidnapped or in danger but rather was leaving a trail for him or someone else to follow. But to where? She clearly was not meandering but headed in a direction to something or somewhere. Could it be possible she knew something he didn't?

In the midst of the fourth Turning the human inexplicably grabbed his tail & was trembling with fear. This was not acceptable behavior for a human, yet he sensed the human knew something. Very strange as he should certainly know anything the human knew! He stopped & questioned the human in their simple language. The human pointed in the direction they were going then leaned over & drew something in the dust of the desert.

Furto leaned over & looked, he had drawn some sort of a creature that resembled a human but had horns & wings on it. Furto had never seen or heard of such a creature, how could this lowly human know about it when he didn't? Yet it seemed outrageous that he would be making this up. What could this mean?

Furto questioned the human best as he could about this creature. The human seemed to indicate it was an old race known as the Wingdits & that their land lay just ahead of them less than a Turning. They were fierce & feared no one & no creature. Furto asked him how he knew this and the human simply said it had been passed down through their generations and this was the place spoken of in their lore. Furto wondered if this was some old fable – but then why would

Parthen be headed right for them if it was just a fable. It seemed he did not know everything & something had been withheld from him!

Furto assured the human he would protect him but that he must continue on. He was searching for another dragon & he would search for her wherever he had to go. He kept thinking about these Wingdits that the human mentioned and could not remember any mention of them in any of the dragon writings. Very strange he thought. None of the dragon lore mentioned them – yet the human lore did & furthermore somehow Parthen seemed to know about them!

Over the next hill they encountered a sign written in Dragon, human & 3 or 4 other languages. It stated: "This land belongs to the Wingdits, you are hereby warned that you enter at your own risk!" So, the human was right! This seemed incredible to Furto – yet the markings continued right into the Wingdits land. He must go on regardless of the risk! The human was now sticking VERY close to him, as bit too close actually!

Suddenly in another quarter Turning they were surrounded by a group of these Wingdits – Furto was surprised at their size, almost as tall as a dragon! They did not seem to take too kindly to his being there. One of them spoke harshly in the human language and said they were not welcome here & were now their prisoners! A dragon a prisoner? That was preposterous to Furto! Dragons may be exiled or killed but were never prisoners!!

Furto replied in the human language to them that he was searching for a dragon named Parthen that had left some markings – which he pointed out to them. First, they were surprised that he knew the human language and then they begin to talk some foreign language among themselves feverously. Furto wondered what this could mean. Apparently, they had been talking to the human initially & not him. Why they would do this Furto could not fathom!

Presently one of them who appeared to be a leader among them came up to Furto and in the dragon tongue inquired.

"Are you Furto?"

Furto was taken aback, how could they possibly know his name??

"I am" he replied after regaining his composure.

"Come – you follow us" He replied a little too gruffly Furto thought.

They followed this group because they really had no other choice and Furto was curious as to how they knew his name. A race he did not know existed spoke the dragon tongue & furthermore knew his name? Where was he? They went on for another half turning and presently there appeared a gleaming city in front of them! It was magnificent to behold and Furto had never seen anything like it! It gleamed golden & silver in the afternoon sun. There seemed to be colored fabric in the windows rich & deep in color. The walls however seemed to be crawling with armored Wingdits. The human was trembling so much he could barely walk now!

The leader gave some signal to the gate guards & the doors opened without any aid. What was this?? Furto went in with them knowing full well he was completely at their mercy now. But he also knew they could have easily just killed them out in the desert if they had wanted to, there was some reason they had not yet been killed. Was he to be a sacrifice at some ceremony? Where was Parthen?

Presently they came to what appeared to be some sort of palace. Beautiful what appeared to be white stone covered the façade. Maybe the ruler of this kingdom? The leader signaled Furto to stop.

"You wait here" he told Furto & left the Wingdits of his company with Furto as he went in alone to the palace. The human was now clinging to his tail. The Wingdits looked on the human with distain – even more than they had for him.

Presently he returned and signaled Furto to follow him. But the human was to stay with them. Furto told them in no uncertain terms that the human was his property & they must not harm him. The Wingdit leader assured him the human would be safe with them. Furto went in and was in awe at the beauty of the place! Beautiful deep colored tapestries, golden & silver overlaid everything. He wondered where they had gotten all this. There was more here than Furto had seen in his lifetime with the dragons. They went in to what appeared to be a throne room like place. As they entered, he looked up and there sat Parthen next to a very important looking Wingdit.

Chapter 3 - Parthen

Parthen had set out after their exile in the opposite direction of Furto. She was so angry with him for getting her exiled! Love her! Hogwash! She told him not to follow her she did not want to see him again! He looked very hurt but did not follow her and instead went off by himself. This was a big desert, but she knew something about this desert that VERY few dragons knew about and she was going to take advantage of it now.

Out on the very edge probably 3 or 4 Turnings distant there was a fierce race of creatures known as the Wingdits she would go to them. First though she must get some strength she would not rush herself but take her time getting there. That first Turning she slept in a hollow in the dusty desert floor. The next day she continued on and found a nice desert tree to sleep under. She grabbed some desert critters here and there to stave off her hunger and came upon a little stream. She drank deeply of it and it refreshed her.

By the start of the third Turning, she began to feel that maybe she had been too harsh with Furto. She made a claw scrap on a rock should he decide later to follow her. By the end of the third Turning, she was placing regular scraps on the desert rocks, but not too close together. She slept that night and dreamed about Furto and wished she had not been so mean to him. He could have easily blamed her. She realized and Symb would have believed him and she would be dead and he would still have been a Shadow Dragon.

It suddenly dawned on her that he must have really loved her! He had given up the most important position a dragon could ever have in order to save her! She suddenly and desperately hoped he would come looking for her and find the clues she left. She could not go back for him now, she had to get to her destination and soon!

The next day she began leaving the scraps at regular intervals close enough to create a trail. She knew her footprints would soon be swept away with the desert wind but the claw marks would remain for a long time. It was now the fourth Turning but she was taking her time and probably had at least another Turning before reaching the Wingdit border. She would rest here a Turning or two before heading into the Wingdit lands. She was sure that she would be welcomed there but did not want to take any chances. She would scope it out a bit before heading in.

Two Turnings later she ventured near what she was sure was the Wingdit border, but did not see anything or anyone. She retreated back to her resting place that night. The next Turning, she again went to the border and carefully observed for a while – as she saw nothing except the desert critters, she moved closer in. Suddenly she was surrounded by Wingdits a half a wing taller than her! She had not known they were so tall!! The leader grabbed her roughly & demanded to know what her business here was!

To this she replied "Sarcona Estam". It had been the code words her mother had given her many Centa's ago. She hoped they still held true today as she was betting her life on them!

At this the Wingdit leader instantly released her & asked in the dragon tongue "How do you know these words?"

"My mother did a great favor many Centa's ago for your Grand Leader and he gave her these words should she or her children ever need a favor in return. She never did but gave them to me. Now I need a favor from the Grand Leader." She replied. She waited while the Wingdits murmured among themselves hoping that this would be enough to satisfy them.

It had been in truth about 200 Centa's, prior to the reign of Symb that her mother had found the Grand Leader in the dragon territory alone. Normally this would have meant instant death for the Grand Leader but her mother was very compassionate (much more then Parthen was) and accepted his story of having been lost from his comrades for at least 10 Turnings. He did not know where he was so her mother had taken him to the dessert edge & given him some food & sent him on his way. Before he left however, he gave her these code words should she ever be in trouble & need help. He said to simply speak them to any Wingdit and they would know what to do.

Presently the leader said to Parthen rather gruffly she thought. "You come with us!" They surrounded her but did not touch her anymore. She was grateful at least for that as these were rough creatures.

As they plodded along, she would see them occasionally step on the little desert critters and thought to herself that these seemed like awful mean creatures her mother had sent her to! She would not step on critters just for the sake of doing so!

Presently they came over a rise & before them lay a grand city of sorts. Well, it did gleam with splendor of gold & silver but in crawled with creatures all over it! The layout seemed a little haphazard too from what she could see. As they approached the gates their leader signaled to the gate guard & the door large doors swung open effortlessly. Parthen thought how interesting – I wonder how that is done?

Following her party into the city they wound their way through the streets. Other Wingdits in the city came out of their "houses" if you wish to call them that, and watched as she was taken through. Some of the younger ones pointed at her but were quickly taken away by their parents. It seems these creatures as fierce as they are, have either a dislike or a fear of dragons she thought.

Soon they stood before a grand castle of sorts. Parthen was intrigued by all this but did not want to say anything yet. Their leader told her to stay with the group and he would return shortly. Half a Turning later he did return and told her to follow him. They entered the castle and Parthen was taken to a grand and stately room. Before her sat a Wingdit who appeared to be someone of importance here. Around the room sat other Wingdits who appeared to be of noble character. All eyes were on her. She felt a little uncomfortable with that. She was a dragon who did not like being around others but rather would be out in the woods by herself.

"Who are you?" the Wingdit on the throne asked her rather gruffly.

"I am Parthen, daughter of Pent" She replied. At the name of her mother, she saw the look in his eye of recognition.

"Who sent you to us and why have you come?" He asked though she thought he said it a little less gruffly.

"My mother said that if I ever needed help or a favor that I should come to your people and speak these words – Sarcona Estam. So now I have come needing a protection." She replied.

"Protection? Protection from what?" He said almost laughing.

"I have been exiled by the Dragon Ruler to this desert. I cannot survive here alone & need help to survive and to learn the ways of the desert." She replied

"You have been exiled alone" He asked.

"No" She replied. "Another was exiled with me but we have gone our separate ways."

The Grand Leader motioned some other important looking Wingdits over and they talked among themselves in a tongue she did not know. Presently the group broke up and the Grand Leader stood up.

Addressing Parthen he said. "My name is Regen; I am the Grand Leader of the Wingdits to whom you have come. My father's name was Dybat, it is he whom your mother saved. It has been written in the royal annuals of this debt. A Wingdit always pays his debts and we shall honor this debt of my father. You shall have residence here with me in the Royal Palace and learn the ways of the desert. You may stay with us for one Centa."

Parthen was not sure if she was relieved at this or more concerned. Afterall these Wingdits she knew nothing about! Her mother had told her very little about them, but most importantly she had told her to be careful around them. She wondered why her mother had said this.

Parthen bowed low – "Thank my lord that should be more than enough time, you have been very generous with me."

Regen signaled and a Wingdit appeared. "She will take you to your quarters." Regen said "In the next Turning or two we shall sit together and discuss what happened to you & how we can help."

"Very good my lord" she replied and with that she left with the Wingdit assigned to her.

Her quarters where not as nice as her home back with the dragons but it was comfortable & cozy. She had a nice window overlooking the city and could watch the daily life of the Wingdits. She could study their habits and learn of their ways. One thing she learned early on – although they were a fierce race, they had a very ordered society and mates were fiercely protected! Over the next 10 Turnings she had many talks & discussions with Regen and even began to learn some of their tongue. He seemed to be very intrigued with human / dragon relationship and often asked her many questions about it. She wondered why he was so interested in this but he never gave her a straight answer, something about several thousand Centa ago something had happened. She didn't understand what he was alluding to.

He also asked her about the other dragon, Furto and why they had been exiled together. At this point she understood enough about Wingdit society to realize it would be best if she described him as her mate (which in all honestly, she now wanted & was sure he did too), so that if he ever came looking for her, they would save him. Also knowing that she already had a mate out there they would leave her alone (no Wingdit ever messed with another mated Wingdit on pain of death). She had given him Furto's name and description in case any of the Wingdit guard ran across him. This information had been passed on to all the Wingdit patrols.

She had described to Regen what had happened to her and how Furto had saved her and become her mate. Although Regen did not like her description of her flaunting the rules of her society, he did not say much about it. Over time Regen invited her to sit with him in the grand hall. Some of the other important Wingdits had opposed this but Regen insisted. So, she sat with him daily listening to the cases and foreign emissaries brought before him. She had not imagined there were so many races on Xern! Granted many of these races where no significant in any way, but still it she was amazed by it. She was always introduced to them as "Parthen, Honored Dragon". Many of them were quite surprised to see a dragon among the Wingdits, much less in the royal court!

She noticed that Regen was not really giving her any lessons on how to survive in the wilderness and wondered if he really was going to do that at all! There was of course still plenty of time to learn, but she was anxious to start learning! When she asked him about it – he simply said there was plenty of time and to enjoy his hospitality for now. She knew his actions toward her made some of the other Wingdits uneasy. There was little she could do about that.

She continued to daily study the books on Wingdit knowledge & history. She had been given free access to the Royal Library where all the wealth of Wingdit knowledge & history was stored. She begun to find books that mentioned something that happened long ago that she found perplexing. Something about an interbreeding of the humans & dragons. She would have to study this more & press Regen for more of an explanation on this. For now, she was more concerned with learning the laws and ways of the Wingdits. She had been with them now for over 10 Turnings. She now felt safe & comfortable with them.

One day as she sat with Regen in the royal court there appeared a Wingdit guard leader coming in with great urgency. He bowed and Regen asked him what his business was.

"The dragon Furto has been found at our borders and we have brought him here" he replied. The royal court went quiet at his words. One dragon was enough and now there was a second one here! They all knew who Furto was of course and also knew that he was bigger & more powerful than Parthen.

"Bring him in" Regen commanded!

Shortly thereafter Furto appeared at the entrance to the royal court and Parthen let out a gasp. She never thought she would see him again. This time however she was overjoyed to see him though she did not show it yet. At that moment Furto looked up and saw her there.

Chapter 4 – Reunion

A million thoughts raced through Furto's mind! How was this possible? What was Parthen doing here? She looked as though she had been here for a while – had she known about this place and come directly here? On and on they went racing through his mind. As he stood there transfixed Parthen got up and started coming toward him. Why? She had said she never wanted to see him again! Furto was so confused he just stood there transfixed.

Parthen attempting to control her emotions got up and walked toward Furto. It was important that the Wingdits actually believe he was her mate. Both of them would be in a great deal of danger if they even thought for a second they were not mated. She knew enough to know that it was expected for Furto to embrace her & question those in the court as to her chastity. This was not going to be easy. Wingdits expected that to be done but to be done with decorum not like the humans did.

As Parthen approached Furto she bowed and then rubbed the crown of his head (she had told the Wingdits in the past that this was a sign of affection among mated dragons – which it was).

She whispered very quietly hoping no one would notice "Furto the Wingdits believe we are a mated pair, for our safety you must act the part."

At first Furto was puzzled & momentarily there fluttered uncertainty in his eyes. Could this be the Parthen who had stormed off several Turnings ago?? It did not seem possible to him! Then just as quickly he regained his composure – there would be time for questions later. He picked her up in a strong embrace & rubbed the crown of her head. Parthen looked around, it seemed the Wingdits were accepting this. Whatever the consequences Furto was going to act the part. If Parthen was playing some kind of game – so be it. He had come for her & he would not back down now.

She whispered quietly again to him – "You must ask about my chastity while you were away."

Furto put Parthen down and addressed Regen.

"I do not know the ways of your people O great one, but I must ask you has Parthen been kept safe for me from all others?"

Regen smiled – "You have my word Furto, she has had no other."

"Parthen & I have much to talk about your highness, is there somewhere we can go & talk privately?"

"You can go to Parthen's quarters, which are yours now as well. You will not be disturbed there. But do not miss the royal banquet tonight."

Furto nodded and Parthen lead the way out of the court.

"It is only a short distance to my quarters Furto. We can speak freely here; I have much to tell you."

Furto nodded again uncertain how freely they could really speak. Parthen lead him through several passages & archways each time they passed the royal guard they gave way to them. Finally, they arrived at a stately room & Parthen closed & bolted the door behind them. The room was regally arrayed in fine linen & exquisite paintings.

"Come Furto we have much to catch up on"

She led Furto to the sitting room where the afternoon sun was shining in.

"Here my love drink some of this tea it will ease your tensions."

Furto took a few sips when suddenly he realized he had left his human in the outside court!! This would not do!

"Parthen I must go back to the court – the human Symb gave me is still there!"

"Don't worry Furto – the human will be safe there. Come now we have much to discuss." Parthen knew that in the Wingdit society property was almost as sacred as a mate. Thievery was almost unknown in their society!

"Are you sure Parthen? Symb would never forgive me if anything happened to him!"

"Furto, I have been studying Wingdit society over the Turnings that I have been here, property is fiercely guarded & thievery is nearly unknown here." Furto was amazed at these words! These creatures seemed so fierce & war like yet they seemed to have a strict & orderly society.

"Parthen how freely exactly can we speak here?" Furto asked.

"These walls do not have ears Furto anything you say will only be known to me. I can assure you of that on my mother's skull!"

Furto relaxed just a little with those words. For a dragon to swear on his or her mother's skull was to swear on their life.

"So, tell me what has happened that you have changed so much in relation to me?"

She began to tell him everything she knew starting with her mother & Regen's father. How she had been told of this place by her & the secret code word she had given her. She told how she had resented Furto for making her an outcast – but then realizing on her walk here that he must really truly love her. She told how she had begun leaving marks on the trail leading the way hoping that one day he would find her. She told him of her arrival here & the kindness that Regen had showed her. She told him of the studies of the Wingdits she had done. She left nothing out. Finally she said:

"Furto – If you don't love me for what I have done to you I understand, but I want you to know that here & now I do love you!" She hoped that he could forgive her, she had been so stubborn & thickskulled and caused him so much grieve and heartache.

Furto was stunned at this and all that she had related to him. How could he not love her! He wondered about her mother Pent – he wondered who she was, somewhere in the back of his mind it seemed that named rang a bell. He couldn't quite place her, but it seemed she was a dragon of importance.

"Parthen – I will never stop loving you know matter what you did or will ever do!" Furto stated emphatically and it was true.

"Then it was no lie I told them we are mated! For we are! Tell me everything that happened to you since we separated. I want to know it all!"

So Furto started at the beginning telling of his disappointment & how it hurt him when she left him after their exile. He her told of his days looking for food & hanging out in the cave. He told of his decision finally to go find her & how he would never forgive himself if anything had happened to her. He told her of going to the border & finding Jabas there & of the honor Symb had given him. He told her of his search to find her & the shock he experienced just earlier today! She let him speak without saying a word. When he was done, she said with a tear in her eye -

"Furto, I don't think I can ever make up to you for all the hurt I have caused you. I can only ask your forgiveness for not seeing who you really are."

"Parthen, I forgave you long ago for this. Now it is time for us to move on. I hope that from now on no matter what happens we will move on together."

She took him in her claws & embraced him, rubbing her crown vigorously on his crown. Furto slowed her down –

"There will be time enough for that later my love. Now you must prepare me for what awaits at this banquet that Regen speaks of. I am not sure how to behave or what is expected of me!"

Parthen knew all too well what was going to happen at this "banquet." This was going to be the test of their loyalty to each other. Banquets were always tests in Wingdit society & this was to be their test. She did not know what form the test might take though! The Wingdits had all kinds of inventive ways to test creatures! Some more severe than others.

"Furto – the most important thing I can tell you about this banquet is that it will be a severe test of our loyalty to each other. You must remember at all times that no matter what "appears" to be the case you must remain loyal to me. Only then will you pass the test." She could not emphasis this enough. Dragons rarely tested other dragons, but Wingdits often tested each other. It was part of their warlike society.

"We will furthermore be expected to be wearing the finest that the royal court offers us. I will call the royal courtier in shortly who will find you the finest attire – you will be expected to appear as a warrior." As all males in Wingdit society were expected to be at any social gathering.

"Will you not be tested too?" Furto asked

"Yes" Parthen replied "I will be put through the same tests of loyalty that you are. Both of us must past the tests! If either one or both of us fail it will spell disaster for us." She did not tell him that they would likely be tested separately and maybe even in different ways.

Furto thought about all this, wondering what sort of test the Wingdits had invented for him & Parthen. Shortly there was a knock & a courtier appeared & motioned Furto to follow him.

"Go my love, do not be afraid and remember what I told you." Parthen said.

Furto followed the courtier to another room not too far away. There were all kinds of dress in this room all made for Wingdits. But the courtier found some armor and a spear of regal quality and draped some fine satin and gold wraps around his body. Furto assumed the courtier knew that he was doing & just accepted whatever was given him.

"When you enter Regen's presence you must bow low. You must never embrace your mate in his presence!"

Was this part of the loyalty test Furto thought? Had they not already embraced in his presence? Furto simply nodded when the courtier said this.

"Soon it will be time to go – Parthen will meet you at the banquet"

Furto looked in the mirror and contemplated what tonight would bring. He had no doubt that whatever the outcome good or bad

Parthen would be by his side. But he still had a lingering uneasiness about all this. It seemed almost surreal to him. Wasn't it just hours ago that he was on the desert floor surrounded by these Wingdits and now he was "dressed" in their finest attire! He wished he had more time to talk with Parthen and this "banquet" had been later. Well best get it over with whatever happens tomorrow was another Turning if he survived this, which he was not at all sure he would.

Chapter 5 – The Banquet

As Parthen prepared herself for the banquet she thought about all that Furto had told her. She steeled herself for what she knew from seeing others that his would be a grueling test of their loyalty. Wingdits unlike any species she had ever known enjoyed seeing others suffer; it had been a tough several Turnings to live among them. Up to now she had not been tested, but tonight she knew the test would come. She put on her finest satin & gold dress took one last look and headed to her fate.

She headed down the hallway to the great banquet hall. Upon entering it was strangely quiet. She wondered where everyone was. A lone figure stood at the end of the great table, Regen himself. He beckoned her forward.

"I am sorry my dear Parthen, Furto cannot be found. He seems to have left the royal courts & left no word. Do you know where he is?"

She was momentarily taken aback. She had expected a test but not this strong & not so soon! She knew it was a test however. She did not reply but simply stood where she was.

"Come Parthen" Regen reached to touch the crown of her head.

"Do not do such a thing Regen! You know I am mated to Furto!"

"But he has abandoned you Parthen!"

"I do not believe you Regen, Furto would never abandon me even if the Orb stopped turning!"

"Ahhh but he did abandon once not so many Turnings ago!"

"He did NOT abandon me – I shamefully abandoned him. That will NEVER happen again!"

"Yes, but he could have followed you right away could he have not?"

She did not know how Regen knew all this detail about their exile – it was a bit unnerving to say the least. She had not told him everything maybe he surmised some of it. She must not waiver she MUST remain strong!!

"The ways of the Wingdit mates & the dragon mates are not the same Regen – surely even you will acknowledge this."

"Yes, but I saw a hint of shock in his eyes this afternoon when you met, surely that is not the way of your mates?"

So, he had seen & noticed that earlier today – how much more had he noticed that he was not yet divulging to her! She would have to make something up fast and hope they did not ask Furto the very same question!!

"He was shocked that his mate would be in the presence of another species Regen – we dragons are a solitary species as you well know!"

Regen made another attempt to touch her and this time she backed several steps away to keep distance between them.

"Where is Furto? I know you know where he is Regen! Nothing enters or leaves this palace without your knowledge. I have not been here these past 10 Turnings without knowing that much. Besides that, where are all the other guests?"

"I do not know where Furto is" Regen replied "As for the other guests they will be arriving momentarily"

Parthen did not believe Regen – she knew he knew where Furto was. So, this was their game – they were going to grill them separately. Well, that was a new twist on things more like what dragons would do really.

"I must go now to welcome the guests. Stay here & the others will join you shortly." With this Regen left the banquet hall.

Parthen wondered if this was part of the test. Should she stay or go looking for Furto?

Meanwhile Furto had been pacing back and forth wondering why he had not yet been called to the banquet! He was getting impatient! He knew that was one of his worst faults.

As he was about at the end of his patience in walks Regen.

"Oh my you do look fine tonight Furto! Come we must not keep the guests waiting."

As they walk Regen asks casually "Tell me Furto what was that shock I saw in your eyes earlier today. Surely you would not be shocked to see your mate?"

Furto contemplated this question wondering how he should answer. He wondered if Regen had already asked Parthen this question or was going to. He took note that the Wingdits notice everything no matter how small. He could do nothing but hope that the answer he gave would be similar to Parthen's. He had no way of knowing that Regen had already asked her & the answer he gave was identical to hers!

"I was not shocked to see her, but as you may not know dragons are a solitary species & do not interact with other species all that much. This is what shocked me in that moment."

Regen seemed satisfied with the answer.

"The banquet will start soon & the guests are arriving now." Regen said as they entered the banquet hall. Furto looked around but did not see Parthen anywhere.

"I was told Regen that Parthen would meet me here. Has she not arrived yet?" This seemed strange to Furto, all dragonkind was punctual!

Regen looked around "She seems to have not arrived yet – I will send a courtier to check on her" At this Regen signaled a courtier who scurried off.

"Don't worry I am sure she will be here." Regen said with a smile that Furto did not trust. "In the meantime, make yourself comfortable and sample some of the appetizers." Furto suspected this was part of the test as well. Parthen had told him that a Wingdit mate never eats until his mate is present. At least she had told him some things! It was so hard to keep it all straight!

"I am sorry Regen – I cannot eat until Parthen arrives!"

"Suite yourself!" Regen replied casually.

Presently Furto saw the courier return. He spoke a word with Regen and presently Regen came over to Furto.

"I am afraid Furto that we can't find Parthen!"

"She is not in her quarters & a search of the palace is underway."

That was enough! "You LOST Parthen" Furto roared!

Furto immediately stormed out of the banquet hall. He would find Parthen if these incompetents had lost her! He knew the way to her quarters just a short distance from the banquet hall. Entering her quarters he saw that she was not there – but when he turned around there was a contingent of the guard waiting there for him.

"No one loses their temper with the Grand Leader. You will be tried immediately for high crimes against the Grand Leader!"

Furto did not know what this meant but they bound him before he could react and led him away. So, this was how it all was going to end, some trumped up charges & he would probably never see Parthen again. Well so be it, his heart was broken & he had no will to live.

Regen reentered the banquet hall and found Parthen still there.

"Come Parthen. That Furto is up to no good and is immediately to be tried for high crimes."

Parthen did not know what to make of this. It could not be true! This was surely a more severe test then even she had imagined! She followed Regen to the royal court where they had been just hours earlier today and where she had felt such joy at the return of Furto!

Regen motioned her to sit next to him where she had so many times before & had been earlier today. Then he motioned to one of the court Wingdits & in came Furto in chains surrounded by armed guards. She could not believe her eyes. Surely this could not be happening!

"What is the charge" Regen asked the guard.

"High crimes against the ruler of the Wingdits" was his reply.

"What is the high crime" Regen asked.

"Speaking with anger to your majesty" was the reply.

Oh no Parthen thought – she knew Furto was impatient at times and might very well have done this. He had no way of knowing this was so serious an offense! She trembled as the words were being spoken. She should have told him about this, but she had no time to tell him everything about Wingdit society. O why had they not given her more time!

"The sentence for high crimes is death" Regen said callously.

Furto bowed his head there was nothing he could do now. He saw Parthen there with Regen & his trust in her waivered. So, after all this – after all this searching – after all this giving up of who he was it was going to end in a simple ignominious death! He almost could not bear it. After loving and wishing for Parthen all his life, now when he had her it was being ripped from him! He could not even protect her from what these base creatures would do to her!

Suddenly there was a deafening roar in the court! Furto looked up – could that have really come from Parthen?! Such a small dragon making so loud a roar – he never heard her speak this way!

"He does not deserve this! I deserve it! I will not allow this court to proceed! You will take my life for his! If you do not then I will hang myself!" Parthen said. She knew that hanging herself would case disrespect to the ruler & the court and they could not allow it.

"NO PARTHEN" Furto roared! You will not take my place! I will pay for my crimes!

Regen saw that chaos was ensuing and needed to regain control! The Wingdits in the court did not know what to make of this! Never had they seen a display like this some were running around with their wings up in the air some were flying around (which they rarely did even though they could)! It was total chaos in the royal court!!

"SILENCE" Regen roared!

"Very well" He said – "according to the laws of our land another Wingdit may step in for the life of another, but it may never be the mate of the accused."

Another test thought Parthen – he wants us to admit that we are not mates. Stay strong Furto! She stared into his eyes willing strength to him. He seemed to regain his composure. But he also seemed to be wavering in his faith in her. He seemed like he was giving up and didn't want to live anymore.

"Your majesty" she began "While Furto is my mate; you have taught me well in the laws and customs of the Wingdits and have allowed me access to all the writings of your people. What you say is true; however there have been instances in the past when mates of other species have been recorded to stand in for their mates when no other of their species was around."

"Parthen, you have learned of our people well. What you say is true. Therefore, I will allow you to stand in for Furto. But as you also know the receipt must agree to allow it. Furto, do you allow Parthen to stand in for you?"

This Furto knew was a test. He however did not know how to answer. If he said yes, it could well be seen that he did not really love her. If he said no then it could be seen as a sign of disrespect to her. Finally he replied:

"I do not wish to show any disrespect to you Regen or to my mate Parthen. I cannot however allow her to stand in for me. My love for her is too great to allow this to happen. I do not know how your people show it, this is the dragon way."

Instantly Parthen replied "I will therefore plead equal justice"

Equal Justice was a law of the Wingdits. It required when plead that the law see both mates as equally guilty for whatever crime had been committed. Once plead it was irrevocable and therefore very rarely used. Furto did not know what this Equal Justice law was but he could guess. He was amazed at how versed Parthen was with the Wingdit laws.

"Very well" said Regen – you have pleaded Equal Justice & all the Wingdits here are witness to it. "Take her with him to the courtyard"

Furto saw that when they entered the courtyard, they were to be executed by the old human guillotine method. Very well at least it was quick. The guards motioned him forward; he presumed he was the first to be executed. He quietly placed his neck in the slot and waited. Just as the guillotine was to be released, he was shocked suddenly felt her neck on top of his!

Regen then shouted "STOP" with not a second to spare.

In the next instant his chains were released & the guards disappeared. Suddenly Parthen realized this was more a test of her loyalty then his! She also realized they had passed the test. This was all to see if she would be loyal to her last breath. She was exhausted & could see that Furto was too.

"Come my love we have passed the test."

Furto was both mentally and physically exhausted from this. He had all he could do to get up. He did not know how Parthen did not seem as exhausted as he was. Maybe she had just been better prepared for it. They had both been through the most severe test she had ever seen the Wingdits give. But the important thing was they had passed the test. They would not be tested again at least not for their love for each other. Wingdits only tested once for anything.

Parthen & Furto returned to what was now their dwelling place.

Chapter 6 – Questions

A couple of Turnings later after Furto & Parthen had slept & eaten well enough to recover their strength again they received a request from Regen for a meeting. Furto did not know what to make of this, but was not ready for another confrontation.

"What do you think this mean Parthen" He asked.

"I do not know my love, but I do know that the laws of the Wingdits do not allow for a second test." She replied.

Furto looked around and noticed that his human had been placed in their quarters with them; he looked well enough and not abused at all. Well that seemed to be a good sign. Furto addressed him in human's simple tongue.

"How & when did you get here? Are you alright?"

"Yes, I am fine. They have treated me well on account of you & your mate. I was put in here by the guards two Turnings ago. Both of you looked totally exhausted so I did not bother you. I have been told to give you whatever you request during this time until you recover." The human replied.

"Furthermore, the guards have assigned a royal courtier to me so that anything I thought you needed could be supplied swiftly. I have been requesting those meals which I know will give you strength and help you recover. Is there anything that you need now?"

Furto shook his head – this all seemed so surreal! A royal courtier being assigned to a lowly human! This seemed so preposterous! But on the other hand, the humans knew well the dragon diet so it was probably a good thing they had done this.

"No, we have need of nothing else right now" Furto replied "Unless you can provide us with some information." Furto would not normally ask a human such a thing, but things were so confusing here and this human seemed to know stuff that Furto did not. Would hurt to ask he figured.

"What kind of information do you require?" The human asked.

"Regen has requested a meeting with us – do you have any information what this meeting is about" Furto asked.

"I am very sorry; I do not have any information about that." He replied

Furto thought that the human did know something though and was holding back. Maybe he was afraid of the Wingdits if he said anything. Well, it was not worth pressing the matter now.

"Very well you will remain here while we go to meet with Regen as he has requested us." Furto said. The human nodded agreement.

"Are you ready my love?" Furto asked.

"Yes, I am ready. Regen requested we meet him in the Great Court before the end of this Turning, so we should hurry and not make him wait." Parthen replied.

Furto and Parthen strode side by side as was the dragon way, down the hall toward the Great Court. It was not a long walk but Furto took his time, he was in no rush to get to this meeting! As they approached the Wingdit guards bowed and opened the doors. Now this was new thought Parthen, Wingdit guards bow to no one except the royal family! She did not say anything but could see the surprise in Furto's demeanor.

Furto just did not know what to make of all this! The last few Turnings had been such a huge up and down he was just exhausted trying to figure it all out. He saw that Parthen appeared modestly surprised and gathered that this was not normally what the guards would do. He wondered what it all meant!

As they entered, they saw that Regen was seated at the royal table filled with all kinds of foods. No one else was in attendance or anywhere to be seen and the guards closed the doors behind them. Regen motioned them forward and asked them to sit with him.

"Now here is the promised banquet" Regen said.

Furto was too weary still to say anything, but Parthen replied. "You are very generous with us Regen, the test you put us through was most severe, we still are weary from it."

"I want you to know that I know you both are in fact not mated."

Furto and Parthen instantly both tensed up. What could this mean and how did he know after they had passed the test? Both were immediately concerned for the safety of the other. Regen saw this and replied.

"Do not be afraid at these words. The reason I know is because of the code words you gave me Parthen. I cannot tell you why at this time, but will tell you both that you have done very well and have nothing to fear from any Wingdit in my realm!"

"Only myself and a very few other trusted Wingdits know the truth. As far as everyone else is concerned you are a mated pair. Do not fear me or my trusted Wingdits we know the truth but also know that you have passed the test and therefore deserve the respect as a mated pair would receive."

Parthen relaxed just a bit. Another of the Wingdit laws stated that an unmated pair who passed the mated test was to be regarded in all respects as if they were mated.

"While you recovered a degree has gone out throughout my realm that you are to be given the highest respect as if you were in fact a member of the Wingdit royal family. Anyone who violates this decree will pay with their life."

Furto thought this was a bit severe, but then he was quickly learning that Wingdits always did things to the extreme. Well that explained the guard's behavior Furto thought, but it did not explain why they were being treated like royalty. He was missing something here. He would have to question Parthen later about those words and where she got them from.

Parthen meanwhile was thinking the same thing and wondering what exactly those words meant that her mother had given her. She was beginning to think the Pent had not told her everything.

"Regen" Parthen said "We are honored that you have elevated us to this level, neither of us is a dragon of any great significance so it seems rather odd to us to be elevated to such a level! It seems the code words my mother gave me have more meaning than what she told me. Can you tell us anything more?"

"I cannot tell you any more at this time. You will both find out in time the whole meaning and what it means for your futures. I just want you to be at peace and know that you will be well treated from this time on."

With that Regen motioned them to eat and changed the subject to more mundane things of the realm. Parthen wondered at the words "your futures" it seemed a bit enigmatic! Clearly Regen knew a lot more than he was telling them. But why? For what purpose was he not telling them everything? The rest of the banquet went uneventfully and soon it was time for them to leave. After thanking Regen for his generosity, they left.

Back in their room Furto questioned Parthen about the code words. She told him everything she knew and what her mother Pent had told her about them. At the mention of Pent Furto seemed to recall that name. He would have to try and remember why he knew her. Something about Symb's dad seemed to ring a bell with that name.

He and Parthen decided they should do a search and see if they could find any information on the words 'Sarona Estam.' There had to be something here that would tell them more. For now, they both decided to sleep and check into the library next Turning. Furto saw that his human was fast asleep. Furto curled up next to Parthen and soon fell fast asleep.

Chapter 7 – The Report

Jabas had been waiting at the outpost now for some time. He was alone with his thoughts here being only one of three dragons that manned the three outposts. No other dragons other then Symb knew of the existence of these outposts. He was glad he had convinced Symb to send that human with Furto. Symb rarely denied him anything anyhow. This particular human was very well known to Jabas & had learned many things humans were not normally taught. He would be able to help Furto & send word when the time was right.

There was only two Wingdits, the three dragons, Symb & Regen that knew of the existence of these outposts. Over the last several Centa they had been very carefully developed and sometimes crucial political decisions had come about as a result of them. Just a Centa ago the Wingdits were ready to go to war with dragons over a misunderstanding. Jabas & his Wingdit counterparts had intervened as a last-minute effort by Symb & the war had been averted. Dragonkind had not known how close they came to war.

Looking up he saw the two Wingdits he knew well approaching quickly. I hope they bring some good news Jabas thought to himself. He left the outpost to greet them as they approached.

Jabas slightly lowered his head and said in the Wingdit tongue.

"Hail honored Wingdits"

They likewise slightly lowered their heads and replied in the dragon tongue

"Hail honored dragon!"

"Do you have some good news for me?"

"We do indeed" they replied

"Very well then come into the outpost here and we will dine while you tell me of it."

Jabas over the years had become accustomed to these official meals – he knew what his guests liked and always had some of their favorites on hand. They were as he and many other dragons considered them a base race that liked to eat their meats raw. It was disgusting to Jabas but for sake of this alliance he did what was necessary. They also loved the dragon wine! Wine was uncommon in the Wingdit kingdom so it was a treat for them to have it here.

"Now" Jabas began "Tell me everything that you know."

"Sarona Estam phase I is complete!"

"O that is indeed good news my friends (not really but it made them feel good)."

"The test Regen devised was the most severe in all of Wingdit history. He was duly impressed with Furto. Parthen has been with us for 20 turnings and has learned the laws of the Wingdits very quickly – her mind is sharp."

"What more can you tell me about Parthen – Symb will want to know everything?"

"Parthen's dedication to Furto and stubbornly adhering to the mating was impressive. During the mating test she pleaded the rarely ever used statue of Equal Justice – this actually took Regen by surprise! He did not expect someone who was not actually mated to claim this statue. It is a testament to how much she has changed."

Jabas had heard of this statue of the Wingdits but was not all that familiar with it.

"Can you tell me about this statue, I have heard of it but do not know that much about it."

The Wingdits then went on the explain that a mated pair of Wingdits may claim Equal Justice as a last resort if they cannot save their mate and do not wish to live without them. This statue can only be pleaded in capital punishment cases. Once the plea has been entered it cannot be changed or reversed. Both mates will receive the same punishment of death. They also explained to him how Parthen at first had attempted to substitute herself for Furto, but Furto would not allow it to happen.

Jabas was stunned! This is the same Parthen that stormed off by herself 20 turnings ago? It seemed incredible that she would do this! Apparently the Wingdits noticed his shocked look.

"Do not fear they were not harmed. It was only a test they are alive and well!"

Jabas recovering himself said – "My friends I was only stunned that Parthen would do this! It just seems incredible – are you certain it is Parthen?"

"Yes, we are certain! She gave us the code words and matches the description you send us exactly. Furthermore, the human verifies it is her."

After this they discussed other matters of state before Jabas sent them on their way with the charge to report back as soon as phase 2 was complete. He had to get all this news to Symb. It just seemed so incredible he was not sure Symb would accept it!

Jabas stood in the courtyard of Symb's palace as he always did when he had news for Symb. He talked with the other dragons that were there making small talk about the weather. None of them knew who he really was not even that he was a Shadow Dragon. Presently Symb came out & caught sight of Jabas there. He momentarily looked up to the Orb. This was the signal to Jabas to meet him in the secret gardens. Presently Jabas said goodbye to the dragons assembled there and headed to the secret gardens.

As Jabas entered, Symb was already there waiting impatiently as he always was. But this time was different. He saw Jabas enter & rushed over.

"What is the news Jabas – what have the Wingdits said?"

Jabas bowed before saying.

"Sarona Estam phase I has successfully been completed"

"Excellent!! This is indeed good news! Did they tell you how it went?"

"You will not believe it sir"

Symb raised his eye flap and Jabas knew he better keep going. Symb was not one who liked a lot of conversation. Just give him the facts.

"I was told that Parthen has studied and learned the Wingdit laws quickly sir. Furto arrived a bit ago and they were both tested as you requested. They were put through a very severe mating test that no Wingdit has ever before endured. Furto as expected lost his temper & was condemned to death."

Symb looked aghast at this and Jabas quickly continued.

"Parthen attempted to exchange her life for his, but according to the laws of the Wingdits Furto had to accept such an exchange and he would not allow it. Parthen then pleaded the Equal Punishment statue of the Wingdits."

At this Symb gasped. "No this cannot be the Parthen that I exiled from here!"

"That was my reaction as well sir! Are you familiar with this statue sir" Jabas asked?

"Yes, I am Jabas" Symb replied. "It is very rarely ever used. Parthen must have learned their laws very well indeed. Still, that is a huge reversal of course from the day she left us here."

"Have no fear though sir the Wingdits assure me on their mother's wing that no harm has come to them – it was only a test as phase I dictated."

"Thank you Jabas – you may return to your duties now. Let me know if there is any word from the Wingdits or the human we sent with Furto."

Jabas bowed and left the secret garden. He returned to the Shadow Dragon quarters. It would likely be some time before phase 2 was completed and he had some work here to do. Jabas was tired and needed some sleep; he curled up on his bunk and was soon fast asleep.

Chapter 8 – The Search

Furto & Parthen had now been searching through the records of the Wingdits for some time now and had found absolutely no reference to the words Sarcona Estam. It was very strange as everything the Wingdits knew was recorded. They apparently were very diligent record keepers. All this searching had taught them a lot about the Wingdits however. They were very dedicated to family but punishments for wrongdoing were equally as severe. Community was important to them & festivals (which were many) were expected to be attended by all. Still, they could find no reference to these strange words which apparently their soldiers knew about. It was frustrating and Parthen was growing tired of searching for the answer – she was impatient to learn of the desert and how to survive there.

Seven Turnings had passed when Regen summoned them to a private meeting.

"My courtiers tell me you have been searching the royal archives and spending much time there every day. What is it that you seek so intensely? Maybe I can be of service & help you find it sooner."

"Sir" replied Parthen "We have been searching for any reference to the words Sarcona Estam. We want to learn more of these mysterious words and what they mean to the Wingdits."

"You will not find anything written about them Parthen. Those words are dragon words and were given to my father by your mother Pent. As was requested at the time there has been no written record of them. They have been passed down by word only."

At this Parthen & Furto looked shocked. How could this be? These were not any dragon words that either of them had ever heard. They did not even resemble their language.

"Very well then" Parthen replied "I wish to start my training in desert survival soon and I presume that Furto will now be part of that."

"As you wish Parthen, tomorrow we will begin Furto & your training."

Furto could not let it go though. "Regen, why can you not tell us more. You know all about them but leave us in the dark! We are dragons, we deserve to know everything you know about this!" Furto crown bristled as he said this.

"You must trust me now Furto, it is for your own good. You will in time know everything, but for now you can only know what I have told you."

"Come Furto" Parthen put her paws around him "We will talk of this another time. Let us go out tonight & enjoy the Festival of Darkness. You will be there Regen, won't you?"

"I will be there Parthen."

Later as the Orb waned in the sky the festival began. Furto thought this is a good opportunity to talk to some of the Wingdits about this word. He had become obsessed with finding out its origin and meaning. He would ask some of the palace guard & maybe he could even find the captain that had taken Parthen at first when she uttered the words.

As they weaved their way through the festival goers no longer in fear as the Wingdits had for some time now seemed to accept them being in their presence and no longer feared or threatened Parthen & Furto. The dark blackish drinks they had at this festival Furto never liked but Parthen would drink some here & there. Soon they came upon one of the palace guards – obliviously off duty tonight and a bit tipsy. So Furto took advantage...getting his attention Furto asked.

"How is it that you and your fellow guards know the words Sarcona Estam and what do you know about them??"

The guard instantly looked alarmed.

"Do not ever again utter those words in public!" He looked nervously about to make sure no else had heard them.

"What do you know?" Furto persisted.

"I do not know anything about them. We have been sworn to protect the dragon who utters them. We have not been told why or what the meaning is. They are to remain a secret & must never be uttered in the presence of the common Wingdits."

This only made Furto more intent on finding out about them. Everything he learned just seemed to add to their mystery. Furto continued to mingle with the crowd with Parthen, but his mind was elsewhere. He could not shake the feeling that he and Parthen were in some kind of game. Something was not right and he had to figure it out. Obviously though tonight would not be the night. Regen was being very mysterious and suddenly he got the feeling that only Regen knew the truth of those words.

Tomorrow would be another day and Regen had promised to start desert survival training. This was important as they would have to go out on their own sooner or later. Best he and Parthen turn in early and get some sleep!

Chapter 9 – Initial Training

Parthen awoke as the orb was swinging around its low point. She was alarmed when she found that Furto was not next to her. She quickly got up only to find that he was nowhere to be found in their quarters! This was their first day of training – where had he gone! She was concerned as he had left no note and had not done this since arriving here.

Furto seemed rather sluggish to the Wingdit guards. He has been awakened quietly in the wee hours and hurried quietly out of his quarters. Furto was still half asleep and put up no protest at the time. Now as the orbs light began to brighten once more, he was becoming alarmed at what had happened. He had been transported out into the desert and now was in what appeared to be empty trackless desert; he could not even see the city! What had happened??

"What is going on?" Furto asked the Wingdit commander in charge.

"Your training has begun" He replied. "Soon Parthen will also be out in the desert with her detachment of guards, your first job will be to locate each other."

"What? How will I do that?" Furto replied in incredulously.

"We will give you this bit of advice" replied the commander "listen to your heart it will guide you to her."

This seemed crazy to Furto – they could be several Turnings apart and he was to listen to his heart as if it could tell him anything about her location? Stupid Wingdits he thought. Furto was startled when the commander said "It is not stupid dragon, but you must learn the ways of desert on your own. We will not be far away, but you will not see us." With those words the Wingdits uncharacteristically flew off. Great thought Furto, now they have left me here in the middle of nowhere with nothing in sight to go on! Stupid Wingdits! They probably just want me to die here – maybe that is best anyway he thought.

Parthen got up and decided to see if she could find Furto somewhere in the royal palace. Maybe he was having a talk with Regen. She opened the door, only it wouldn't open! It seemed it was locked or barred from the outside. What was this? She was a prisoner now? Moments later the door opened and an escort of Wingdits entered.

"We are to take you to your training Parthen." the commander said.

"Why was I locked in here?" Parthen asked.

The commander did not reply but simply motioned her to follow them. She was not inclined to do so without Furto.

"I cannot leave here until I know where Furto is." She said firmly.

"Furto has begun his training, the first phase of your training will be done separately" he replied.

This did not sit well with Parthen. Ever since Furto had returned to her he had been her rock and she had felt safe. Now it seemed like Regen was conducting yet another test! When would this ever end!

"I do not feel comfortable with this" she replied – even though she knew Wingdits had little concern for 'feelings.'

"Do not delay us" the commander replied "You will soon be back with Furto if you come with us and your training goes well."

She had little choice in the matter so she indicated to them to go and she would follow them. Out they went in the still early orb light of the quiet streets. Out of the city gates and into the desert, further and further they went until not even the city was visible it had been almost a full Turning when they stopped. She wondered what lay ahead; she hoped following the advice of her mother had been the right thing to do. The commander turned to her...

"Now begins your training, the first order of training is to be able to locate your mate. Furto is out here to with the same information as you. You are to locate each other. Our only advice to you is to listen to your heart. You will have three Turnings to find each other. Do not attempt to retrace your steps. You will get lost as all traces of our coming here have been removed. Follow your heart. We will not be far away but you will not see us."

With that the Wingdit guards flew off and were gone. First, she thought what will happen if we don't find each other in three Turnings! She presumed that they were within at least three Turnings of each other. Listen to your heart...listen to your heart...listen to your heart. Her heart was not saying anything to her. But that was all she had to go on.

Furto continued to mull over what life meant and why bother with all this anyhow. Symb had thrown him out here anyhow, after he had done so much for him! He sat down to mull over all this and consider his options. He was exhausted and soon fell asleep. The next moment it seemed that Parthen was coming to him! Parthen here – over here he said – but she did not seem to hear him or see him and just flew on by him! Wait, what? She flew! Did Parthen really fly? The next moment he woke up startled! It was just a dream – but it seemed so real! The words of the Wingdits came back to him – listen to your heart!

He closed his eyes again. Then he seemed to be flying himself over the desert! The sensation was incredible – dragons were meant to fly he thought to himself! Then off in the distance he saw Parthen sitting on a rock. He flew toward her – but again she did now seem to see or hear him. How strange he thought to himself! He folded his wings and landed next to her, still she did not seem to see or hear him – almost like he wasn't there. He reached out and touched her and she jumped and looked about afraid. With this he woke up again. Is this what the Wingdits meant thought Furto?

Parthen was sitting on a rock mulling things over when she felt something touch her; she jumped aside but did not see anything. What were the Wingdits up to now she thought? It had been a long Turning and she need some sleep, she was not sure she felt safe but had little choice. She found a cove like rock to curl up in and fell asleep.

Suddenly she was flying! Wait what? Swooping through the sky in her mind, but it seemed so real! Then she saw him – Furto flying also above her – she tried to get his attention, but he didn't seem to see her. Frustrated she flew toward him but he disappeared over a mesa. She flew over it but did not see him. Listen to your heart came back to her thoughts. Listen to your heart...listen to your heart. She was startled when she felt she should fly to the right and down into a valley there. There she saw him sitting on a rock seemingly dejected. She landed next to him but he didn't seem to see her. She reached out and touched him and he jumped much as she had earlier. Suddenly it dawned on her – this is what had happened to her earlier. It had been Furto that touched her! Furto had found her in his dreams! Now they had to find a way to recognize each other in their dreams. She awoke moments later – but with a new excitement at what she had realized and found. If he came to her again, she would acknowledge his presence and see what would happen!

Furto meanwhile had been sitting on a rock in a valley thinking about what all these dreams meant and even if they had any bearing in reality. Obviously, she could not see or hear him so it was likely just a dream and nothing more. At that moment he felt something touch him and jumped aside but did not see anything. The desert was a desolate place that played tricks on your mind he thought. Well, he had not made any progress in finding Parthen yet, those damn Wingdits where probably laughing their heads off.

Commanders report to Regen – Turning one: Furto has made a little progress but does not trust his heart. Parthen has listened to her heart and is already nearly in touch with Furto. We do not know what will happen when she makes contact with him.

Regen read the report and knew that this would probably happen. Furto was not the type to go on feelings. Wingdits were not known for their feelings either but at times they were needed and survival in the desert necessitated them. He hoped that when Parthen made contact Furto would be accepting of it.

Furto was feeling tired – it had been nearly 2 Turnings since they had left him here. Another day of scrounging through the desert had yielded him nothing. This damn place was so devoid of anything useful! He slammed down his claw on a rock and a little lizard scurried out. He grabbed it & downed it with one gulp – well at least he had something to eat!

Finding a secluded rock shelter, he curled up and tried to get some sleep. Suddenly he was flying again. Damn dreams taunting him with something he could not do! As he soared over the desert, he once again saw Parthen curled up and apparently sleeping. He thought about just going on, but something deep inside told him to go to her. Why he thought, it is only a dream & she will not see me anyhow? Almost against his will he landed beside her.

He reached out to touch her as if some unseen force was moving his arms! Her eyes fluttered but she did not move. She looked in his direction then said very quietly...

"Furto is that you? I cannot see you but I know that you are here. I came to you earlier today and you felt me but did not know it was me. We have now found each other but we need to figure out how to see each other."

Furto was astounded! Could it be that it was her that had touched him earlier? Furto thought – if she can't see or hear me – maybe she could see if I wrote in the sand. So, he began to write in the sand that it was him – but he felt that he was only in a dream. She watched as he wrote, then she wrote with her claw that she was so happy to have him there. She said that maybe in dreams is how soul connections are made! He wrote in the sand that they should begin to move toward each other and gave her the direction he was. She nodded and immediately set out in that direction. Furto flew back and made a notation in the sand near where he was in case he forgot the direction when he awoke.

Later Furto awoke but could not remember the direction he had come from and where Parthen was. Then he remembered he had made a notation in the sand. O yes there it was! He immediately set out in that direction.

Commanders Report to Regen – Turning two: It appears that Furto & Parthen will indeed find each other very soon. Parthen was the first to recognize what was happening in her dreams then Furto was creative & found a way to communicate without them seeing or hearing each other. They have not made the dream connection yet. But if they find each other then what are we to do?

Regen to commanders – If Parthen & Furto indeed find each other without the dream connection they have made a great step forward. In this case you will instruct them on the dream connection.

Half a Turning later Parthen looked up and off in the distance she could see a dragon! It had to be Furto! Excited she began to pick up her pace! They would make it inside the three Turnings they had been given!

Furto looked up and saw his Parthen running toward him! He was so relieved and at the same time exhausted from this training exercise! He had no idea however how they were to find their way back to the Wingdit city. It didn't matter though! Parthen was here at last! He swept her up & rubbed his crown on hers and she did his.

"We did it my love! We found a way to find each other!"

"Congratulations dragons" They heard behind them and turned to see the Wingdit guards behind them.

"Although you did not make the dream connection you still found each other & figured out how to communicate! That is a great achievement. No Wingdit has ever done that without using the dream connection."

"As a final part of this phase of the training Regen has instructed us to train you in the dream connection. With this you will be able see & hear each other as if you were there in person."

"Tonight, you will sleep with us as equals and honored guests – we have tents prepared with a feast for you. Tomorrow, we will instruct you in the art of dream connection."

The commanders beckoned them to follow and they did so. Just over the mesa there was a huge tent with gay lights & wonderful aromas. Furto was just too overwhelmed to know what to think of it all, but at least he had Parthen by his side!

Chapter 9 – The Art of Dream Connections

The next morning Furto woke up to a strangely quiet camp. Parthen must have got up early because she was not there with him. Very strange he thought. He got up and went out of his tent, but no one was around. Everything was as it had been last night, but no sign of any Wingdits or Parthen. This habit of the Wingdits just leaving him to guess what was going on was getting on his nerves. Where could everyone be?

He rummaged around and found some leftovers from the previous night to slack his appetite – not that he needed a lot after last night's celebrations! There must be something around here that would tell him where the Wingdits & Parthen were! Glancing at the ground he saw writing in the sand – "Go to the top of the Mesa" it said in the dragon tongue. Was this for him or was it some sort of trap? He was sure it was not there moments ago. Sighing he decided he had little choice and made his way up the Mesa.

As he reached the Mesa there was Parthen in a sort of stupor just floating above the ground! What was this? He raced toward her and then right through her! She was not here this was some sort of dream or apparition? What was going on? Was he actually awake or not? Questions raced through his mind as he turned toward her again. She was still there looking at him – had she turned? She was looking at him when he came in from the other direction. He slowly circled around her and she always faced him as he circled. He reached out to her but there was nothing there – at least nothing tactile that he could feel.

It was time to find out if he was dreaming or not. He reached down and picked up the largest rock he could pick up. He was just about to bash his head with it when Parthen suddenly glowed extremely bright, so bright that he dropped the rock right on his tail! It could feel it and it hurt really badly! He pushed the rock off his tail and wondered what he should do now. Apparently, he wasn't dreaming. They must have started the Dream Connection without him and this must be some part of it.

The Wingdits were supposed to be helping him understand this – but he did not see any of them in sight. Useless as usual! Well now he could see her, but had no idea if it was actually her and still had no communication with her! And no idea how she was appearing to him like this! He decided to go back to camp and see if he could find out any information on which direction everyone went. As he neared the edge of the Mesa suddenly a wall of light rose up around the Mesa blocking his exit in all directions! Now he was trapped! He tried to touch the wall but it impenetrable and would not allow him through.

He had to think. Now he was surrounded by a wall of light with Parthen just looking at him. That was all he had to go on. He decided he would try something different. He closed his eyes and walked toward Parthen. At the moment he surmised he was upon her he was swept up into the sky and Parthen was there.

"You have made the Dream Connection" she said!

"What? Where are you Parthen?"

"I am in the Wingdits Royal palace"

"I do not understand how I saw you there or what that wall of light was"

"What you saw there was my sentinel that I put there"

"Sentinel?"

"Yes, when you build a Dream Connection you place sentinels for the other to see and connect with."

"But why did it only sweep me up after I closed my eyes?"

"That is the way they work my love. We knew you would figure this out. Now it is time for you to build your own sentinel"

With those words he was dropped back to the ground. He looked around and the so-called sentinel was gone as was the wall of light. Great here he was again without any instruction and supposed to understand this sentinel stuff! He was too tired for all this, he decided he needed a nap! He closed his eyes & soon he was flying once again over the desert. Off in the distance he saw the Wingdit city and decided to fly over that direction. Why did it seem that Parthen was always given the lessons before he was! It annoyed him and he decided instead to fly away from the city.

Somewhere in his mind he heard Parthen speaking.

"Land on the ground and speak to the Orb to build you Sentinel"

Furto was not keen on doing this. All this mystic stuff was neither his style nor the style of dragons for that matter. Speaking to the Orb just seemed so foolish. That withstanding he did as she told him. He landed on a nearby ridge. Put his feet on the ground raised his hands to the Orb and said:

"Blue Orb of the great sky build me a Sentinel here"

In a flash of blue light there stood floating above the ground was a likeness of himself! He was utterly astounded, how could this be?

At that moment he awoke and was back on the Mesa again. He had no idea where he had built that sentinel or how long it would stay there or how to remove it or how many sentinels he could build! So many questions raced through his head! This was the all-important Dream Connection that the Wingdits had spoken of? Well, it didn't seem that important to him!

Moments later the Wingdits came up over the Mesa and indicated it was time to return to the city. He had no idea where he was and was happy to follow them back – if that indeed was where they were taking him!

"Furto" said the commander "You have done well, all your questions will be answered by Regen himself. We know you do not see the point in this, but you will with time."

Furto said nothing but followed them. He just wanted to be by Parthen's side again. Later that Turning they entered the city and went straight to the royal palace. Regen & Parthen were there. Parthen ran over to him and rubbed his crown in greeting. Furto just wanted some rest and Regen said they would talk in the morning. Parthen & Furto went to their quarters and slept.

Chapter 10 – News

Jabas had received word that the Wingdits wished to meet with him at the outpost. While he waited for them there (he always was there before them) he thought of all that had occurred in the recent Turnings, Symb was getting older now and soon it would be time to appoint his successor, Jabas only hoped that his successor would be ready. Only Jabas, Symb, Regen & the two other Dragons with Jabas knew who the successor was to be. It was being kept in the strictest confidence!

Soon he saw the puff of dust off in the distance indicating that the Wingdits would be here soon. He hastened to the entrance to give them his usual greeting. He hoped they had some good news to give him.

Jabas slightly lowered his head and said in the Wingdit tongue.

"Hail honored Wingdits"

They likewise slightly lowered their heads and replied in the dragon tongue

"Hail honored dragon!"

"What is the news you have today?" He asked them.

They removed a scroll and gave it to him. It had Regen's seal on it. This is from Regen himself & he has asked that be given directly to Symb.

"Do you know what it contains?" Jabas asked

"We do not know what is written there." They replied but we do know that Furto & Parthen are progressing rapidly through their training. In fact, Furto accomplished something no other Wingdit has ever done! Jabas was not surprised by this – Furto although hardheaded still was very inventive when he needed to be. Still, he was curious to know what Furto had done.

"What is this that he did?" Jabas asked

"He was able to communicate with Parthen and reunite with her in the desert without making a Dream Connection." In all the annals of Wingdit history that has never been done before! They seemed genuinely impressed by this.

"Furto is a very intelligent dragon and this does not surprise me. You will see many more things he will do that have never been done before. He may not be easy to get along with but he will always find a way to get things done."

The Wingdits nodded their heads.

"Make sure Symb gets that scroll as soon as possible. Regen will be waiting for a reply."

"I will take it to him now. Meet me back here in two Turnings."

Jabas headed back to the Royal Palace thinking about all that had transpired in the last 50 Turnings. So much was at stake here, so much could go wrong! He wondered what was in the scroll, but also knew that Symb would tell him anything of importance. He tucked in safely in behind his armor plating. It would take ½ a turning to get to the Royal Palace and another ½ turning to return. That left only 1 Turning for Symb to reply. He sincerely hoped it was enough time.

As Jabas entered the courtyard he began to mill about with the rest of the dragons there – presently Symb looked down & saw Jabas there and knew he had some news to give. He looked at Jabas & then to the Orb. Presently Jabas left the courtyard and Symb headed for the secret gardens.

"You have word Jabas?" Symb said impatiently.

"I was given this scroll to give you sealed with Regens seal. The Wingdits say they do not know what is written on it only that Regen was waiting a reply. I told them to meet me back there in 2 Turnings. I hope that is enough time for you to formulate a reply."

Symb broke that seal and opened the scroll right there. His eyes widened and he bobbed his head up and down as he read. Then he gave the scroll to Jabas.

"Here read for yourself. I will have a reply ready in ½ a Turning."

Jabas took the scroll. There was very little written on it.

"THEY ARE READY" In bold letters and written below it.

"I have consulted with my closest advisors; the Wingdits will fully conform to the terms of Sarona Estam." Jabas looked up at Symb. So, this was really going to happen! Jabas looked into Symb eyes & he looked tired.

"Meet me on the next Turning and I will have the sealed scroll for you to return to Regen."

"As you wish sir, I will be here early."

Jabas left and returned to his bunk for some sleep. He wished Symb would sleep but knew he probably wouldn't.

Symb returned to his royal palace and thought about what he would say to Regen. Coming to this moment in time had taken a lot of preparation. He would not tolerant anything getting in the way now. He was ready, the Wingdits were ready – the time was now! He composed a carefully worded reply.

"Regen most exalted leader of the Wingdits! You have done excellent work with Parthen & Furto this will not be forgotten. The time has come for us to execute the final phase of Sarona Estam. Please return Furto & Parthen to the desert entry to which they were exiled. Then have your royal counsel ready when the word is given." He took and sealed the scroll with his royal seal.

Next Turning he met with Jabas & handed him the sealed scroll.

"It won't be long now Jabas" was all he said.

Jabas headed immediately to the outpost where he was to meet with his Wingdit counterparts. As usual he arrived there before they did! They would be here soon he suspected. Soon he did see the tell-tale signs of their arrival. After the usually greetings he handed them the scroll.

"See that Regen follows the instructions within 5 Turnings."

They nodded their heads & hurried off with the scroll. Well, they didn't hang around this time like usual. Must be Regen urged them to return quickly. Jabas returned to the outpost. His work was done for now, might as well relax & have a drink.

Regen read the reply to his letter and nodded his head. The time had come and he was ready to do as had been asked. Parthen & Furto after 20 Turnings had completed all their training and were ready for what lay ahead. He believed Symb had chosen the right dragons to do this! He would return them to the exile point in 5 Turnings but for now they would stay in the royal palace with him. Furto though tough and sometimes hard to get through to and also distrusting was also very brilliant. Parthen though not very brilliant was trusting and learned new things very quickly. They would make a wonderful pair and complement each other very well.

He would have another banquet in their honor tomorrow! He called his courtiers to have them began preparations. He still could not disclose to anyone or them what the purpose of all this was, but that didn't stop him from throwing a banquet for them!

Chapter 11 – The Banquet

As Parthen & Furto entered the banquet hall they noticed that this banquet was unlike any other banquet they had been to here in the Wingdits land. This banquet resembled a dragon banquet much more than a Wingdit banquet. Parthen was excited & happy to see this, but Furto wondered what this meant. What was Regen up to now? It had little time to contemplate it as the lords of the Wingdit realm were filing in and organized like the dragons would be rather then like the Wingdits always were. Furto wonder when all this confusion would finally end, he was tired of constantly guessing what was going on!

"Come, here" they saw Regen motioning to them.

Furto & Parthen strode over and Furto gave him the customary Wingdit bow.

"From henceforth you will no longer bow to me Furto" Regen said without the slightest explanation as to why. He glanced at Parthen but she did not seem to comprehend or just accepted what he said. Sometimes she was just so frustrating!

"Why do you say such things" Furto inquired. "You are my Lord now & I properly must acknowledge that"

"I cannot say why except to say that tomorrow by sunset you will know."

"Please come & sit by me here"

Furto took a seat next to Regen and Parthen by his side. He was tired of all these mysteries and just wanted it to end. Regen seemed to be indicating that something momentous would be happening tomorrow. He hoped it wasn't even more mysteries that seemed to swirl about him & Parthen these turnings.

Parthen thought – I wish Furto could just enjoy the moment more. Look at all these wonderful delicacies the Wingdits have prepared for us! She took some laid out on the table before them and with loving eyes fed some to Furto. One day they would have a little one of their own. Little did Furto know how soon that would be she thought to herself!

Everything was ordered so nicely in the fashion of dragonkind it was almost like they were back home in the royal palace. She wondered for a moment how Wingdits knew the fine details of a dragon banquet! Like how the wine was laid out first then came the meat eaten with delicacy (unlike the Wingdits who even in royal banquets just consumed it with gusto). All the lords in attendance seemed to be following the dragon banquet etiquette. So very strange she thought.

Presently after the feasting had gone on for a while Regen stood up and raised his wings. At this the banquet hall fell silent.

"Lords of the realm of Wingdits, honored guests and dragon friends, tomorrow we leave for the desert gate. Tomorrow we will fulfill & finish the requirements made by our forefathers of Sarcona Estam. Parthen & Furto will accompany us there." The Wingdits present drummed their wings in agreement. It seemed they all knew about it, but he & Parthen did not. This aggravated Furto a great deal. He knew there was much Regen was hiding from him. Why were they being taken to the desert gate when Symb had exiled them there many turnings ago? This could not possibly end well. He needed to see Jabas!

Furto quietly left the banquet telling Parthen he was not feeling well & would return after he rested a bit. That human Simba gave him would now prove his worth. Furto found him in their quarters and instructed him to send a quiet message immediately to Jabas. The human acknowledged his instructions & went off immediately. He did not know if Jabas would even get the message & reply before morning. In any case he would return to the banquet for now.

Chapter 12 – The Return

The next morning too early for a dragon to wake up there was much commotion outside their quarters. Furto rolled over to see Parthen already up & about. She looked different today, glowing almost. He rubbed his eyelids must be something he drank last night! He had not heard from Jabas last night – so he would have to go into this whole thing blind. He hated that. Last night had been long & the rivalry too much for him. He looked at Parthen.

"You look positively happy & glowing this morning. I don't know how you managed that after last night." He said.

"Oh, I just can't wait to get back & see my homeland again!"

"Doesn't it strike you as odd that Regen is taking us back to where we were exiled without any explanation as to why?"

"Yes, that does seem a bit odd but Regen only has our good in mind!"

Just like her to think that. He for one could not depend on any Wingdit to do the right thing. Just then there was a knock on the door.

"Come in" Parthen said sweetly.

Furto's human opened the door & entered.

"You have word?" said Furto

"Yes – Jabas replies to follow the instructions Regen gives you."

Jabas is in on this too Furto thinks to himself.

"Thank you – you may go."

"What was that?" Parthen says

"I sent a message to Jabas last night."

Before Parthen could ask any more questions the Wingdit courtiers were at the door. The time has come to prepare to leave. You need not bring anything with you except the traveling items you will would need, they were told. Again more strangeness! Furto was getting so tired of this, but for Parthen he did as they asked. It would take two turnings for them to reach the desert gate. After packing a few things, they followed the courtiers out to the royal palace. Again, everything was laid out in dragonkind fashion. The processional which featured all the lords of the Wingdits & the entire royal court were apparently coming with them! What in the orbs name was going on? Nonetheless the lords & royal courtiers were assembled as per the requirements of dragonkind – not as Wingdits usually did. They were escorted to an ornate royal carriage where Regen was waiting for them.

Regen seemed excited – this was not at all like him.

"Come Furto & Parthen, everything is assembled & ready to go."

"Once again I ask you Regen what is this all about."

"Once again Furto I cannot tell you. Soon VERY soon you will know though."

Regen then gave the signal & the procession started to move out of the royal palace. At this pace it would take at least 3 turnings to reach the desert gate! They must have been up before dawn to get this all ready. Maybe they didn't even go to bed last night! Wingdits flapped their wings at them as they passed through the streets of the city. Some called out Parthen's name as she had been known to some of them. Furto figured most of the processional would leave them when they left the city & entered the desert. He was wrong & groaned to himself at the slow pace this would mean through the desert.

"Regen, most dragons don't even know of your existence, what will happen when we get to the desert gate and they see all of this." He said pointing to all the Wingdits with them.

"Do not worry Furto. The plan is in place. You must trust that this is for the good of dragonkind & Wingdits."

The plan is in place? What plan thought Furto. Near the end of the first Turning the procession found a place to camp for the night & laid out their campsite with Parthen & Furto in the places of honor. They set up an elaborate tent for them spacious enough for them to be comfortable in. Furto just wanted to sleep. But first he said to Parthen.

"Parthen, will you go with me tonight in our dreams? Will you follow me? Don't ask any questions though."

Parthen looked perplexed but nodded that she would.

Furto fell asleep then. He waited for her & saw her coming. He pointed to the sky & they took flight together. He flew toward the desert gate. It was strangely desolate. He kept flying toward the dragonkind palace. Then he saw them. The lords of dragonkind, the Shadow Dragons & other imperial ranks as well. All were marching toward the desert gate with Symb leading out. He was worried, very worried were they headed into a war? He looked at Parthen she appeared a bit worried too. But if there was war – why were no warriors of the dragon's present? It did not make sense. He motioned her to return, and together they went back to their tent.

Furto woke up the next morning refreshed from a good night's sleep. Parthen once again was already gone off somewhere. He poked his head out of the tent and could smell breakfast cooking. Somewhere out there Parthen had to be!

Parthen popped her head around the corner.

"Come on Furto they are breaking camp & waiting for you to get up! We have some delicious breakfast cooking for you!"

Furto glanced around – they must have been up before dawn again! They sure seemed in a hurry to get going! Furto got up & stretched and looked in the mirror. Well might as well get going to whatever lay ahead. No sooner did he leave the tent then the Wingdits started taking it down! Breakfast sure smelled good though!

After breakfast Furto & Parthen again got in their carriage & the procession got underway. As they plodded through the desert Furto continue to wonder what this all could possibly mean! Parthen seemed to be taking it all in stride and he wondered if she really knew more than she was letting on. She snuggled up next to him & closed her eyes peacefully as the procession continued on.

Later that evening they set up camp again. Again, Furto asked Parthen to fly with him in their dreams again tonight. She agreed again. Together that night they again flew to the desert gate. This time they saw the dragons had already arrived. They had elegant tables and thrones set up. Furto could not figure out what was going on. He saw Symb addressing the dragon lords but could not hear what he was saying. He saw Jabas there next to Symb. He looked at Parthen & she shrugged – she had no idea either.

"Lords and Ladies of the Dragonkind" Spoke Symb to the assembled group.

"Tomorrow is a new day for dragons. A long & secret alliance will be completed & fulfilled. Many of you are wondering why you have been commanded to come out here to the desert gate. You need not wonder any longer. There lives out here a race known as the Wingdits. My late sister & the reigning sovereign of the Wingdits father made and alliance many Centa's ago. This alliance will come to fruition tomorrow. A deal was struck with them only known to myself the Wingdit Sovereign and a few very select dragons & Wingdit guards. The Wingdits will teach us how to fly again & in exchange we will be there sovereign lords and protectors of their realm."

"You must now agree to this alliance – tomorrow you will learn more."

Next morning as the light dawned once again Furto found himself alone in the tent and could smell breakfast again. Well, these Wingdits did know what made a good dragon meal! He got up and headed out to eat. This morning the Wingdits did not seem in a hurry, they must be near the desert gate he thought. Regen came and bowed before him. Not this again Furto thought.

"My lord the time has come – today is the day! Will you permit me to travel with you today?" Regen said.

Since when did Regen ask him permission to do anything, thought Furto? But he nodded his consent and Regen joined them in the carriage. Awhile later Regen stood up and commanded the procession to stop.

"Lords of the Wingdit race today just over that hill lies the desert gate to dragonkind. You have been called here to fulfill the terms of Sarona Estam. Many of you wonder what that is – a few of you know. I cannot tell you with Parthen & Furto here – Symb wishes to tell them himself." With that he motions to the Wingdit guards. "Furto & Parthen will you consent for a few moments to be put in insolation so that I may speak with the rest of the Wingdits?"

Furto thinks what does it matter at this point. He has no clue what is going on anyhow! Parthen demurely agrees. Furto nods and the guards place a large heavy tent of some kind over them. It is however light on the inside but they hear nothing from outside.

Regen continues. "Honored & noble Wingdits. We have made a solemn alliance with dragonkind. Once again, we will be allies & not enemies. Under the terms of the agreement, we will teach the dragons how to fly again, they will be our lords over us but also provide protection to us. They will allow us our lands and we will live in peace once more. I will be your lord but under a dragon sovereign lord. You must agree to these terms now before we proceed."

Presenting the tent was lifted and Regen motioned them to rejoin him in the carriage. Well, whatever lay ahead it was going to happen VERY soon thought Furto! As the carriage crested the hill & started toward the desert gate Furto could not believe what he saw!

Chapter 13 – Sarona Estam

Symb addressed the assembled lords of dragonkind.

"Momentarily the lords of the Wingdits will be coming over that hill right there. We will formally enter our agreement which you have agreed to last night."

As Furto crested the hill & looked down every lord of dragonkind was there waiting just beyond the desert gate. They all had on their formal regalia as if some kind of coronation was about to happen. The procession halted just before the dessert gate. Furto saw Symb & Regen then move forward toward each other.

"It is good to finally meet you have all these Centa." Said Symb

"I am honored to meet you." Said Regen in flawless dragon tongue.

"Have you lords agreed to the terms." Symb asks.

"They have" replied Regen. "And have yours?"

"They have also." Symb says "Very well then bring Furto & Parthen here."

Regen & Symb return to their respective gatherings. Regen says to Furto & Parthen –

"The time has come – follow me."

Furto not knowing what else to do follows Regen with Parthen by his side. They enter through the desert gate & see Symb waiting for them. As they pass the lords of dragonkind they bow to them. Symb is waiting for them on his throne at the far end of the walkway. There are two empty thrones next to him. As they approach Furto bows & Symb beckons him to sit next to him on the empty throne and Regen to sit next to him. Furto is done as is requested & Parthen stands behind him. The Wingdit lords are they asked to come through the gate & stand with the assembled dragon lords. Symb than stands and addresses the assembled lords.

"A long time ago my sister was patrolling the outer edges of our land. She came upon a Wingdit that had strayed into our land. This

Wingdit asked for mercy knowing the laws of our land. My sister who always had compassion asked who he was. She then found out he was the ruler of the Wingdits. Upon this discovery she told him who she was. She told him she wished to negotiate a peace agreement with the Wingdit race. Thus, was born Sarona Estam known only to a few. Under the terms of the agreement one day our races would be at peace. She spared his life & today his son stands before us ready to fulfill the agreement. Under the terms of this agreement, we will provide a dragon that will be the ruler over the Wingdits but in an administrative capacity only. This dragon will be approved of by the Wingdit lords. The Wingdit rulers will continue in their capacity in all other things. The dragon who rules them will be the heir to the dragon throne. The Wingdits under these terms will teach dragons to once again fly.

Now I know many of you are wondering who will be the ruler of the Wingdits & heir to the dragon throne. First let me tell you that Parthen is my sister's daughter." Symb then looks at Furto.

"Furto you are hereby proclaimed to be the Wingdit ruler & heir to the dragon throne! Everything that has happened to the both of you up to this point was meant to test you. We needed a special dragon to begin this new era. Parthen you were being tested as well. The dragon ruler & his mate must be true to each other and have complementary traits."

Furto is aghast he cannot believe what he has just heard! So, all the last 30 or 40 turnings where just a test? He was assigned to Parthen just to test him? He feels light headed – this is too much! He sees everything spinning then it goes black.

Parthen rushes over just as Furto keels over. Some of the dragon healers rush over & administer some healing herbs, but Furto does not come to. Regen motions to the Wingdit healers & Symb allows them to come near. The Wingdit healers administer a special oil to his forehead, his eyes began to flutter. Parthen is still holding him in a tight embrace. Furto wonders what just happened then sees all the assembled lords

& remembers. He feels weak. He sees Jabas there smiling at him. He wonders how much Jabas knew.

"My lord Symb – I do not know what to say. This is so overwhelming. I am at a loss for words."

"You need not say anything right now Furto. The Wingdit lords have agreed to accept you as their ruler as has Regen. The dragon lords have agreed to accept you as the heir to the throne. You will rule here when my time is up. Until then you will rule over the Wingdits. They will begin to teach you & Parthen how to fly again."

Parthen smiles – so Symb is her uncle! She always knew she had royal blood in her! She feels happy & ready to burst with excitement. She knows how Furto must feel though & decides to curtail her joy for his sake.

"My Lord Symb" she says "We of course must have a formal mating ceremony for Furto & me!"

"Of course, Parthen that is planned for the next Turning. All of the lords of dragonkind & Wingdits will be in attendance! But for now, let us drink & eat this is a time of joyful celebration!"

Parthen knows that Furto is probably not all the 'joyful' right now and would just like some time alone.

"Symb – Could Furto & I join you a bit later. This has been a lot for us to take in & we could use a little time to ourselves for a bit. Jabas please join us also."

Symb nods "Of course I understand – but please do join us later."

Jabas nods also "Of course I will join you, I could never say no to my dear friend."

With that Parthen guides the still wobbly Furto to a secluded area outside of the celebration and Jabas follows just behind. Furto looks at Parthen with thankful eyes.

"I can tell Parthen that you just want to go and celebrate but thank you for some moments alone. I do need to gather my thoughts. I wish there had been some sort of warning about what was going to happen."

"Jabas my dear friend, how much did you know about all this?"

"I am sorry Furto, I have known about this agreement for a Centa now. But under the terms of the agreement, you could not know until today. In fact, it is I that recommended you to Symb to fulfill the agreement! I am very proud of you my friend you are the right dragon to begin this new era!"

"Jabas, you have always been true to me through thick & thin. If I ever inherit the throne, you will be my second in command! I promise you that."

"Parthen my beloved, what does this all mean? How much did you know? Please be honest now with me."

"Furto my love, I did not know as much as you think. I did know, at least suspected, my mom was of royal blood. She did tell me if I ever found myself in the desert to go in a SW direction & find a race called the Wingdits & then utter the words Sarcona Estam to them. That is all I knew before today."

"Very well Parthen you still want to go through the mating ceremony with me next Turning? After all this you could still back out now."

Jabas glances at Parthen a wee bit nervous.

"Furto, I will not back out ever! How could think that after all we have been through the last 20 Turnings! You are my mate & always will be!! Besides if I did back out it would violate the terms of the agreement."

Jabas nods in agreement.

"Furto my love, are you ready to join the celebration now? Is there anything else you wish to say Jabas?"

"Yes Parthen, also under the agreement we will be setting up special communication link between the Wingdit ruler & he who sits on the dragon throne. I will explain this to you later but it is nearly complete."

Furto rises, "very well let us join the celebration."

With that the three dragons head to the celebration already in progress. Symb smiles when sees them coming & waves them over to join them. There is every kind of dragon & Wingdit delicacy set before them. The humans are busy serving all the guests. Furto notices that the Wingdits are being careful to eat their food properly. Well maybe we can make them more civilized he thinks!

A special tray is brought to Furto & Parthen containing the most delightful food he has ever seen! Parthen indicates for him to choose first, in true dragon fashion. Well, he better get used to this food as he is probably going to have a lot of it from now on. There is music going on & the humans are dancing, he wonders how long this is all going to go on! The Wingdits are flapping their wings in their fashion of happiness. Sigh was he the only one a bit worried about all this?

Furto grabs some kind of red meat cooked on a bone with some sort of dressing on it. He begins to munch on it & offers some to Parthen. It was very tasty and seemed to have some kind of spice in it. He would have to talk with the cooks – he was not a fan of spicy things.

Later that Turning things begin to wind down. For Furto it had been a long day and he wished to just get some sleep. Parthen, sensing he had enough asked Symb if they could retire & gave them leave to do so.

Symb clapped his hands and humans came running. "Show Furto & Parthen to their quarters!"

The humans lead them to an ornate spacious tent fit for a king. Well, I guess we are going to be treated this way now, he thought. Still not really believing it was true.

"Tomorrow my love we will officially be mated." Parthen said

"Did I tell you Furto that at my request we are to mated in both the dragon mating ceremony & the Wingdit ceremony?"

Furto groaned – great two ceremonies instead of just one.

Chapter 14 – Mating Ceremony

Furto woke up the next Turning, well this was it, today he Parthen would officially be mated! He had always wanted this, but somehow, he felt unsure of it after all that had been going on lately! He of lowly blood being mated to a dragon of royal blood, it seemed surreal! He saw Parthen there beside him & knew it was true though. Parthen's eyes fluttered open and she looked radiant! She came close and rubbed her crown on his. He felt giddy at this and in turn rubbed her crown. They lay there for a while just holding each other. No one outside dared disturb them.

"Well, my love" Parthen finally said "now is the day to fulfill your & my dreams! Are you ready?"

"I am ready my beloved! From this day forward we are now the rulers and will behave as such! I am ready to assume the position given to me with you at my side!"

With that they got up and went outside. Overnight the whole camp had been transformed from a celebratory dinner venue into an elegant royal mating venue! There must have been a thousand humans working on this through the evening Turning! Yet they had heard nothing!

Jabas motioned to Furto, "Come this way my friend, I will assist you in preparing for your mating ceremony. Parthen, my mate Cerno will assist you with preparing you. You will not see each other again until the ceremony begins."

Furto embraced Parthen and they parted ways. Jabas lead Furto to another tent. Inside were Symb & Regen. Furto still not fully able to grasp what was happening stood as Symb placed the sash of state on him and attached an ornate royal sword to his side.

"With these symbols you are officially the heir to the throne. You will wear them always in all official events & ceremonies."

Then Regen stepped forward, he placed a tiara on his head and attached another ornate sword to his other side.

"With these symbols you are officially the ruler of the Wingdits. You will wear them always in public & at all official ceremonies & events."

Furto examined the sash it was of a satin weave with dragons woven of gold thread into it. It had black coloration throughout, indicating him being a black dragon, it also had a blue dragon next to a black dragon near his shoulder of course indicating Parthen his mate. On the hilt of the sword was a finely crafted black dragon. Everything about this indicated him and his new position!

He looked at the tiara in the mirror. Its crest had a form of a dragon on one side & a form of a Wingdit on the other. Inlaid with jewels and made of gold & silver. He had never seen this likeness with the dragon & Wingdit. Regen saw him looking at it and said – "This is the newly christened symbol of our united lands Furto. You are the first ever to wear it."

Parthen was led to another tent. She was given the gold veil of a royal princess and the mating oil. On her was placed a sash of state and in her left claw was placed the scepter of the royal wife. On her head was placed a tiara identical to Furto's (though she didn't know it at that time). She looked in the mirror & nodded. She was ready to go and give herself to Furto. She was led to a small tent at the end of walkway to the mating alter. First, they would have the dragon mating ceremony.

Furto waited while the initial mating ceremony got underway. Symb would come out & welcome the lords to the ceremony then ask if any had an objection to the ceremony. He could hear this taking place right now. After that Parthen would be presented to the assembled guests. She would have to swear on her mother's grave that she had not been mated to another. Next Furto would be brought out. Just then Jabas came in.

"It is time my friend"

Furto followed Jabas out with all the eyes of the assembled lords on him.

"Furto" began Symb "Parthen has fulfilled her obligations & sworn on her mother's grave that there is no other. There are no objections here to your mating. Do you therefore take Parthen this Turning to be your lawful mate? Will you be true to her for the rest of your Turnings?"

Furto looked at Parthen, so radiant & beautiful. "I will"

"You may anoint your chosen mate Parthen."

With that Parthen approached him & poured her special oil over his crown.

"With this oil I make you my mate" he heard her say "No other has this oil and it will never be again." He felt a shiver as she did so and then it was as if he could feel her presence in him.

"I now pronounce you mated" he heard Symb say. "Regen, will you come forward"

As Regen came forward Furto rubbed the Parthen's crown.

"In the way of our race you will now also be mated" Regen said.

Regen motioned to a Wingdit lord who brought up two rings.

"These rings are to be worn around your arms. They symbolized your union together." Furto had no idea how they were going to get those rings over their claws & onto their arms. "Like these rings a Wingdit mating can never be dissolved. Wingdits mate for life and do not tolerate any straying from this. Do you Parthen accept this & agree to adhere to it for the rest of your Turnings?" "I do" he heard her say. "Do you Furto accept this & agree to adhere to it for the rest of your Turnings?" "I do" he heard himself say.

Regen then lifted his hands up to the great Orb and said,

"O great Orb – I now entreat you to mate these two dragons under the terms of the Wingdit mating. Hear me now and perform my request!"

With that the two rings began to change form and text in both dragon speak & Wingdit speak appear on the rings. Then the rings rose of their own accord one came to him & passed through his arm encircling it. The other did the same with Parthen.

"These rings now symbolize your mating. They can never be removed."

Regen then addressed the Wingdit lords

"Do you now accept these two as mated under Wingdit law?"

All the Wingdits fluttered their wings in agreement.

"So let it be written"

Symb then spoke. "I now present to you your accepted rulers O Wingdits and your accepted heir to the throne O dragons!"

All those assembled bowed in acknowledgement.

"We will do all they ask of us!" They roared.

Chapter 15 – The Meeting

Furto was still reeling from what had just happened as they began to pack up & get ready return to the realm of the Wingdits. It all seemed so surreal, he could not believe it was actually real. He kept checking his armband making sure this was real! Parthen kept looking at him wondering why he was so unsettled. She seemed to be accepting this all in stride like she expected it! Maybe it was the royal blood in her he finally concluded.

He tried to help them get ready to leave – but the Wingdits would have none of it and made him go to the royal wagon & wait. Parthen too was not allowed to "help" them either! Parthen came close & laid her head on his shoulders.

"Parthen, why did you accept me as your mate? I have had no rank and came from a family of no consequence. You are of royal blood and should have accepted a mate from the lords of the dragons." Asked Furto.

She lifted her head and looked hurt. "Furto, do you still even now doubt how this can be? You have every quality the dragon lords are looking for to move us forward. In the coming generations royal blood will be of no consequence. Symb has moved as far as he can you have been chosen by the lords to move us forward from here. Do you not know that Jabas is my cousin & the son of Symb?"

Furto was shocked and it showed. He did NOT know that Jabas was the son of Symb! Jabas & Symb had kept this from him (and apparently the dragons in general as well). How could he rule knowing Jabas was the son of Symb & should be heir to the throne! He needed to talk to Jabas now!

Parthen could tell by his look he did not know about this. Parthen said – I have arranged to have Jabas meet us for a private dinner tonight. I suspected you did not know this. You can ask him then whatever you heart desires. We will arrange to not leave until you are ready – remember everyone does what we ask now without question, we only answer to Symb now. With that Parthen left and went to seek out Regen. She found him supervising the dismantling of their quarters.

"Regen – there has been a change in plans. Please erect our quarters again. Furto needs to take care of a few things here before we leave."

"Absolutely Parthen!" With that Regen gave orders to reverse what was being done.

Later that evening Parthen walked with Furto through the cool of the evening to their tent. Arm in arm they went. Furto noticed that when they did this the rings gave off a gentle soft glow. Soon they arrived at the tent and went in. Jabas was already there. Parthen simply said –

"He knows"

Jabas nodded and replied.

"Come the food is ready – let us eat & drink then we will talk."

Furto sat reclined next to Parthen and across from Jabas. He took some of the food but not a lot as he really was not all that hungry considering everything that had happened and what he knew about Jabas now. The food was some of the best he had ever tasted! They ate in silence for a while, though he could still feel a strange connection with Parthen. In his mind suddenly he felt Parthen nudge him. It was almost as if she was saying 'Go ahead ask him.' He looked at her then with questioning eyes. She just smiled back. Did she know about this phenomenon too?

Jabas caught their glances and said "Go ahead Furto ask me whatever is on your mind. I promise you on my mother's grave that anything you ask is okay. I will answer with all truthfulness as Parthen here is my witness."

"I have many questions Jabas but first and foremost is why I never knew your relationship with Symb?"

"From a very young age I knew that I would not inherit the throne, Furto. Symb made that very clear to me. I was not the one to move dragonkind forward in the next generation. I did come to accept this with time. Then my father asked a very important task of me. I was to befriend the dragon who I felt could move dragonkind forward. Don't get me wrong though Furto – You have become & still are my closest friend & I would die for you if necessary! I talked with many dragons & asked the Black dragon master who he thought could do this. Within three Centa of you joining their ranks everyone was pointing to you. I befriended you and after some time agreed with their assessment. I reported this to my father and at that point the testing began.

First you were assigned to Parthen. She did not know who you were or why you were assigned to her. This was done to assess your loyalty. It is important to note that Parthen was being considered as the mate for the next dragon king, she however did not know this.

Next came the test of being separated to see if through being stripped of everything that was important to you, you would continue to remained loyal & protect her as best as you could. Would you also remain loyal to dragonkind. These are important traits in every dragon king not just the new generation. You passed these tests so impressively that Symb was shocked by it! When you came looking for Parthen & met me at the desert gate Symb knew you were going to be the one. But still more testing was necessary.

First if you were going to rule over the Wingdits you would have to learn a lot about them & be willing to be taught by them. This you did though grudgingly – that actual is considered a good trait. It has been considered important that the Wingdit ruler have a healthy dose of distrust. With Parthen being very accepting this balances you both out very well.

The final test came when you and Parthen were condemned to the guillotine this was ordered by Symb though the details were set up by Regen! This was really more of a test for Parthen then it was for you. It was equally important that she be willing to lay her life down for you. You both have come a long way and Wingdit lords have now accepted you as their ruler. I don't think I have to tell you how unprecedented this is!

There was one final test that the Wingdits demanded. You must be mated under their mating ceremony as will all future rulers be required to do. This was accepted by Symb provided you could also be mated as dragons. You are the first mates in recorded history to be mated as such! You accepted the Wingdit mating and so passed the final requirement."

As Jabas finished – Furto laid there stunned at what Jabas had just told him. He knew from what Jabas said that much of it had also been kept from Parthen.

"Jabas my dear friend, I do not know what to say. You will always be my dearest friend. I am honored that the rulers of our dragons felt that I was should move us forward. I will do as best as I can to my ability. Please convey to your father that I will always be true to him and honor his commands! I do not know how you have put aside your right to the throne, I do not think I could be as generous as you have."

"My friend you are my lord now & I accept that! You are the best dragon for the tasks that lay ahead. Over the next Centa the Wingdits will teach you and Parthen how to fly again, then when my fathers time is up you will acquire the throne as it has been written and will return to teach the dragons flight again! Now go my friend – go in peace. We will be in regular contact now. You will return here for the festivals and I and my father will come there for the important Wingdit festivals."

With that Jabas lowered his head and gave Furto da slight bow of respect. Now Furto knew why Jabas had done that so many Turnings ago! Furto placed his claws on Jabas shoulders as a mutual friend would do upon parting. Then Jabas left their tent. Furto looked at Parthen and could see many questions & uncertainties in her eyes. He had not seen that look in a long time. He pulled her close and she willing curled up inside his larger frame.

"Do you know about this mind thing with the rings?" He asked her.

"I have read about my love. It does not always happen. It is believed that only those who are close to each other before the mating this happens to. The rings do not always glow either. The Wingdits believe it is a sign of their allegiance to each other and those that don't glow should seek counsel."

"Tomorrow we will break camp and return to the realm of the Wingdits" Furto replied. "Tonight let join our bodies in the dance of the mated."

Parthen vigorously nodded her agreement.

Chapter 16 – Symb & Jabas

After their meeting Jabas went to meet with his father the next morning.

"Furto & Parthen have been told everything father. Furto though as we expected was a little unable to grasp it all but enough to continue as ruler of the Wingdits. Parthen was a little taken aback but accepting as we also expected."

"Are you okay?" His father asked him.

"I am father. Furto will be much better at this then I could ever be. I am too much of a warrior and too trusting, not as much as Parthen is but still too much for this role. The Wingdits also are too distasteful for me to rule over them!"

"We will make plans to go see them soon Jabas. Have the courtiers arrange something for us in the next 20 Turnings or so."

"As you wish my father."

Now that the Wingdits and the dragons where openly working together it was no longer necessary to send messages in secret. They would simply send a human to them with the dragon flag & the Wingdits would send a human with the Wingdit flag. All the guards knew to acknowledge this.

As the human entered the Wingdit realm he was very nervous! He could be killed at any moment. He held the dragon flag VERY close to himself! Presently five armed Wingdits confronted him! He waved the flag and they lowered their weapons and waved him to come forward. He then communicated with them through his heavy accent that he had a message for the rulers. They then motioned for him to follow them.

As Regen was trying some cases in his royal palace there was a commotion outside and he saw some Wingdit guards enter.

"What is going on" Regen demanded. Irritated that his trials where being interrupted.

"We have here a human who carries the dragon flag with a message for the rulers he claims." They said.

"Bring him forward. What is the message you have" Regen asked the human in dragon tongue.

"It is for the rulers" He replies.

Regen senses it is for Furto & Parthen and sends a request to them. Presently Furto & Parthen enter the royal palace where Regen is. They take their seats slightly above Regen and all the Wingdit lord's bow.

"Okay they are here now human what is it that you have to say?"

The human glances around nervously. He opens a scroll & reads. "I, Symb, request that a festival be given in honor of Furto & Parthen which myself & Jabas will attend within the next 20 Turnings."

Furto looks uncomfortable but Parthen is beaming.

"O, I think that is a wonderful idea!" Says Parthen.

Regen surveys his lords and they all give a slight bow of their wings indicating their assent to this.

"Very well" says Regen "we shall have a festival every 25 Turnings to honor Furto & Parthen! The first will be in 10 Turnings. Return to Symb human with this news!"

Presently Jabas saw the human coming back and let Symb know. They ushered him into Symb's presence.

"So, what did they say" asks Symb.

"They have agreed to your request and furthermore have made the festival to be celebrated every 25 Turnings! The first will be in 10 Turnings."